SPECTRUM

SPECTRUM

a novel

JASON K. MELBY

BOX**FIRE**PRESS

Published by Boxfire Press.

Printed in the United States of America.
17 16 15 14 13   1 2 3 4 5
ISBN 978-1-938191-07-7
ebook ISBN 978-1-938191-20-6

Every attempt has been made to ensure this book is free from typos and errors. We apologize if you do stumble across one and hope it won't hurt your enjoyment of the story. Thanks to changes in technology we can easily correct errors for future readers with your help. Contact us at editorial@boxfirepress.com.

To my mom and dad for their support and my friends for their belief in me. I love you all.

1

This universe is not an old one, nor is it young. Its age can't be measured in the meaningless quantity of years. Its machinations move in turn as the gears of a clock. So much is known, but so much is yet to be discovered even by the wisest and eldest.

Deep at the very center of all creation there is a place a few chosen call the Unworld and in that dark place, beings of great power gather to decide the very existence of everything.

At the foot of a great mountain along that desolate plane, a figure stood. He was tall and lanky. His posture betrayed his youth. His skin glistened with power and an aura of divinity radiated from within. He was a god. A young god, but a god nonetheless.

"I'm here! What do you want, Sanctum?" he called up to the mountain. A great hole broke in the rocks above him and two large red eyes burned out of the darkness. Two giant mechanical arms exploded from the ground and surrounded the young god.

"Sur Reel!" Sanctum's bellowing voice came from everywhere. "You have been called to answer for charges of misconduct!"

"What charges? Who charges me?"

"I do!" A lilting voice called from above. Sur Reel looked up and saw Hither, one of the Angelics, floating down. Her wings spread wide from her body and she was covered with ribbons of silk that flowed around her body seemingly of their own will. Her golden hair was long and swirled around her beautiful face as if in a halo. She landed softly but with great purpose. Her eyes found Sur Reel quickly and she looked upon him with great anger. "I charge you with gross misconduct," she said. Her voice echoed with a metallic vibrancy and her words hit Sur Reel's ears as daggers into his brain.

"What misconduct?" he asked. Hither held her hand out and light began to form on her palm and the light then spun quickly and formed a model of a large solar system. The small planets spun and revolved around each other just as they had done in reality.

"The Suurean galaxy. It was the cradle of enlightenment. Those who called it home were destined to bring about an age of peace throughout the entire universe. Their civilization would have brought about literal miracles that would have saved the lives of trillions across the galaxies!" she said. "Until you came along and flicked the moon Sobus into the sun. That act set off a chain of reactions that destroyed every last living thing in that entire galaxy!" Her glare burned brighter. Sur Reel smiled nonchalantly and shrugged his shoulders.

"I was bored," he said.

"You murdered an entire galaxy! Worse than that, you cost The Design a civilization that would have helped countless others grow and thrive!"

"I'm the god of chaos! What do you want? It's what I do!"

"ENOUGH!" Sanctum rang. Both Sur Reel and Hither cowered at his force. "I have heard enough! Hither. I accept your charge against Sur Reel."

"What?" Sur Reel squealed.

"Silence! I am at a loss. We bestowed upon you the gifts of a god, and this is how you deem to use them? To indulge in childish antics at the expense of countless lives?"

"Uh, not countless. I counted them myself. Sixty seven trillion, eight hundred and seventy three billion, nine hundred and ninety eight million, three hundred and fifty nine thousand, eight hundred lives." Sur Reel said proudly.

"I'll tear him apart right now!" Hither hissed. Her wings shot out and she was about to pounce on him, but Sanctum caused the ground to quake and halted her rash action.

"No, Hither. That is not the way," he said. She fell back and looked up to Sanctum.

"Yes. I know. I apologize," she said and then looked to Sur Reel. "To you, Sanctum."

"Look," Sur Reel began. "This is all fun and what not, but we're not getting any younger here. Can we just get on with the lecture so I can pretend I've learned a lesson and we can get on with our lives?"

"No. Sur Reel, you have conducted yourself in actions that are in direct violation of The Design. Your lack of experience in your charges not withstanding, you shall be punished."

"If I may, Sanctum?" Hither said.

"What is it?"

"I have been communing with The Design and I have found something. An anomaly."

"What sort of anomaly?"

"I'm not completely certain. I do know that it could prove to be powerful enough to destroy The Design completely."

"Why do you bring this up now?"

"I think perhaps it would be helpful if we had someone who could investigate this anomaly on our behalf."

"Indeed it would, but I..."

"I propose we send Sur Reel," she said. Sur Reel looked to her.

"Send me where? What are you two talking about?" Sur Reel asked. Hither pushed past him and closer to Sanctum.

"I have been studying this possible catastrophe for a while now and while I can't tell you what it is, I do know where it will start. The planet known as Earth."

"Earth?"

"In the Milky Way galaxy."

"Oh, right. That place." Sanctum said with a tone of indignation.

"Whatever your feelings for Earth and its inhabitants, this anomaly could pose a threat to everything we have been charged to guard. It is our duty to stop it." Hither said. Sanctum's eyes narrowed.

"You wish to send Sur Reel there?"

"Yes. He could live among the mortals and report back to us when the anomaly presents itself. Perhaps we may be able to prevent it."

"Whoa!" Sur Reel said sharply. "Me among mortals? No way! I can't stand those little shaved apes!"

"I agree with Hither!" Sanctum said at last. "You shall be sent to Earth and you will report to us when this anomaly can be properly identified."

"This isn't fair! Aren't I entitled to a trial or something? A jury of my peers?" Sur Reel asked. Sanctum's eyes moved in the darkness and fixed on Sur Reel. They began to burn more brightly.

"Trust me, you do not want the others to decide your fate. They would be far less charitable."

"Fine. So, how long am I going to be down there?" He asked looking to Hither.

"I don't know. It could be days. Weeks. Maybe years."

"Years?"

"It's difficult to say."

"And how am I supposed to fit in down there," he said. "I don't really blend."

"That's easy. We'll take away your powers and you will assume the form of a mortal."

"My powers? You think you're taking my powers? There is no way I'm letting you strand me on that mud ball without my powers!"

"You shall be stripped of all but some of your powers." Sanctum announced. "You have proven that you are not yet mature enough to wield what power you already have. Perhaps on Earth, with limited ability, you will learn more responsible uses for your gifts," he said. Suddenly, Sur Reel began to glow and his body began to shudder. He looked to Hither, his face screwed up in confusion. She merely smiled smugly as light began to shoot through his body and quickly cocoon around him. Soon, he was trapped in a great ball of light and it shot straight up into the void above. Hither watched as Sur Reel faded into nothing but what appeared to be a distant comet speeding away.

"Are you certain of this action?" Sanctum asked. Hither looked to him.

"Not totally, Sanctum, but at least we don't have to deal with him for a while."

"True." Sanctum said. "Very true."

2

The drive into Towers City from Blue Haven took ten hours. Jason Randwulf's eyes were beginning to weaken. The sky above him was growing dark and he hadn't studied the maps as carefully as he had intended to so he was having trouble finding the street he needed to turn at. He was cruising down the streets of a small suburb not too far from the main city center. He could see the cluster of skyscrapers that made up Tranquility Square in the distance. The Manicore building was particularly well lit and the dragon statue that sat upon it was clearly visible. He pulled out the slip of paper he had written the address on quickly and did his best to make out the street signs as he passed. The street lamps did not afford a lot of illumination.

As he kept going, he cursed himself for not having taken the trouble of coming to see the apartment before he had rented it. It would have been easy to take a weekend trip to the city to see it and figure out where he would have to go. He was just in too much of a hurry to move. He had lived his entire life in the sleepy town of Blue Haven. He had thought that he would die there working in one of the many cozy breakfast nooks or bed and breakfasts that fueled the towns economy, but after he lost his job at the Main Street Diner, he realized the time had come for him to strike out and get a real life with a real career, and the first step towards that end was to be someplace where there were jobs that could have a future.

Another two blocks and still he couldn't find Stapp Street. The clock on the dash was a few minutes fast, but it was still late and he would still have a lot of unpacking to do once he found his new home. He stopped at a red light and peered over and saw his salvation. The light wasn't very good, but he could make out the first few letters and they matched. He looked in his mirrors and saw there weren't any cars coming up behind him, so when the light turned to green, he made a hard right turn from the left lane. He straightened out and soon he could feel he was on the right track. He saw the numbers on the front of a passing apartment house and he was coming up on the right block and the numbers were going down, as they should have been. He then saw it. He parked the truck across the street from 789 Stapp Street. He rolled the window down and took a look. It was just as it looked in the online ad. It was an old looking brownstone with actual brick and mortar. Three stories high and heavily ornate. According to what he researched, it had been built back in the fifties and had passed from hand to hand over the years. It once was one big mansion but when it was reasoned someone could make more money by converting it into a six unit apartment house, those days were over.

Jason got out of the truck and walked over to it and up the stairs. It was quiet. The tile floor was worn and cracked. The walls were aged and the pipes were visible. It looked really shabby and poorly cared for. He quickly realized why the rent was so cheap, but he didn't care. He looked at the directory to find the unit where the manager lived. Heather Rhett was on the third floor, across from his unit. Jason took a breath and hurried up the stairs as he had noticed the distinct lack of an elevator.

He climbed up to the third floor and saw two doors across from each other. One looked old and from the outline below it, he could see the lights were off inside. That was his. He looked to the other and it just seemed more alive and cared for. He also saw the door was outlined with light. He walked up to it and knocked. A few moments passed and the door flew open. He saw a woman standing before him. She had curly brown hair and wore big glasses. She had a pretty face but her eyes seemed wild.

"Yes?" She asked sharply.

"Heather Rhett?"

"Who wants to know?"

"I'm Jason. Jason Randwulf? I rented the apartment?"

"Oh!" she said as the realization hit her. "Right. It's kind of late."

"Sorry, it took longer getting here than I thought."

"Oh, it's fine. I don't sleep much anyway. You have any identification?"

"Right here." Jason said as he pulled out his wallet and produced a driver's license. Heather snatched it and scanned it carefully. She then held it back to him.

"Sorry, have to be careful. You never know who's who these days,"

"That's fine. Is it ready?"

"Sure. Here are the keys," she said as she held out a small key ring with two keys already attached. "This one's for the door lock and this one's for the mailbox. The laundry room's in the basement and if you need anything else, I'm right across the hall."

"Great. Thanks."

"Don't mention it. I'll see you around. Neighbor," she said as she shrunk back and shut her door.

Jason quickly unloaded what he could from the truck. It was nearly midnight by the time all his boxes had been transferred into his new apartment. It was a sparse little number. Small kitchen. Hardwood floors. Since he was on the third floor he had a nice skylight. His cell phone began to ring and he reached for it.

"Hello?"

"Are you there? Are you safe?" a frantic voice asked.

"Yes, mom. I'm fine. I just got the truck unloaded."

"Just now? It's so late!"

"I'm not five years old. I can handle being up past midnight, mom."

"I know, of course. I just want to make sure you're well rested. You've got a lot to do. You need to find a job first."

"I've got plenty of money saved up. I'll be good for six months or so."

"I know, but you can't just sit around and let your money dwindle to nothing! The sooner you find a job, the better."

"I will find a job. I just want to take a few days to get comfortable."

"I still don't know why you moved all the way out to Towers City. It's so dangerous."

"Mom, Towers City was voted one of the safest large cities in the country. They have an excellent police force and almost no street crime."

"But they have crime! I hear there's a whole network of criminal organizations out there that you haven't heard of! I read that!"

"You can't believe everything you read in the grocery store check out line, and even if there is secret organized crime, I am going to be as far from it as possible. I don't do drugs and I just don't attract that kind of element. I'll keep my nose clean. Promise."

"I worry so much about you, Jason."

"I know you do, but you don't have to. Not anymore."

"I'm your mother. I'm always going to worry about you. Wasn't that friend of yours a police man in Towers? Tyler?"

"Tyler Zane. Yes, and he was my boyfriend, mom. When he left Blue Haven he came out here and joined the force. As far as I know, he's still with them."

"This wasn't because of him, was it? You aren't just following Tyler around, are you?"

"No! He had nothing to do with my decision in coming here."

"Well, if it's all the same then, I'd like you to call him. I'd feel better if you were being protected."

"I think Tyler has better things to do with his time than protect his ex-boyfriend. He doesn't even know I'm here and that's how it's going to stay."

"Fine. Just know that your father and I will keep your room as it is just in case."

"Thanks, but I don't think I'll be needing it. I think I'll be just fine," Jason said. "Now, I've got a lot of work ahead of me and it's really late."

"I know. I just wanted to make sure you were all right. I'll call you later, but it wouldn't kill you to call here either."

"I know, mom. I love you."

"Love you too. Good night."

"Good night." Jason said and clicked off his phone. He looked around the room at the piles of boxes he had yet to unload. The proposition of going through all of his stuff began to tire him out and instead he opted to just fall face down on his mattress, which had yet to be placed on his bed frame. He tried to sleep, but he couldn't. He looked one way and saw a wall of boxes waiting to be emptied. He looked away and saw his small kitchen and the boxes he had stuck in there. He shut his eyes and the sounds of the city outside began to invade. He could hear the sirens and traffic. The pulse of Towers. He then began thinking about all the things he had to get done. He made a quick mental to do list. He had to finish his unpacking and that shot to the top quickly. The next thing was to find a job. He cringed at that idea since he had never been good at the process of finding employment and he knew it wasn't going to get any better being in a city as large as Towers City. He didn't have much experience and he barely squeaked through the standards of Blue Haven Community college. He had spent most of his working life laboring in the food and service industry so he thought immediately of a job at a restaurant or coffee house. He had researched the market for such jobs in Towers City and he had discovered that the Lauvre, pronounced 'love', Cafe was one of the more hyped establishments. It was located downtown near the business center and was owned by Bethany Lauvre and her brother Tristan. Bethany was the local celebrity of choice. She hosted the most popular morning show on KTWR-TV and was a fixture at all the media events that were held in town. People often accused her of being a vapid nitwit, to which her brother was not quick to deny. It was also noted often how she seemed to love her celebrity more than anything and reveled in it like a pig in the slop. These facts did not deter the fact that getting a job at that cafe would be a great step forward in moving to something more. A celebrity endorsement, no matter who that celebrity happened to be, could carry quite a bit of weight. Jason's thoughts drifted on to the other aspects of his new life. Most notably, his personal life. He hadn't really dated anyone since Tyler and the thought of running into him on the street one day sent a shock up his spine. It wasn't something he had been planning, but if it should happen, he felt it would be prudent to be prepared with something to say. He ran into Tyler on the street in his mind at least twenty times and still he couldn't think of the perfect thing to say. Before he could get to number twenty one, he dropped off into sleep.

3

Jason didn't have a car and he didn't want to waste any money on a cab, so he opted to take his bike into downtown. He studied his map very carefully and made sure to get the lay of the land as best as he could. He found one street that was the vein that led straight up into the city center. It seemed the quickest route so he hopped on his trusty six speed, and zipped off.

He weaved through the heavy mid-morning traffic easily and as he passed into the downtown district, he could barely keep his eyes on the road. Towers City had gotten its name for a good reason. The buildings all around him shot far up into the sky. Towers of glass and concrete were blocking out most of the sun and a lot of sky. The streets were remarkably clean and everyone was in a hurry. People pushed through doors and yelled out to each other as cars honked their horns.

As Jason went along, he could see the rest of the way up to Tranquility Court. That was the main center of all business and social activity during the day. Most of the most powerful corporations in the world called Towers home. Manicore Industries was the largest building in the court. They were surrounded by other equally large corporations, but their building was the tallest and by far most awe inspiring of them all.

Manicore Industries was founded by Augustus Manicore and made everything from Breakfast cereals to biological weapons. Their headquarters housed some of their research and development facilities but there were rumors flying that there were other secret labs they used throughout the city, including an underwater complex at the bottom of the bay.

They had their main world headquarters built in Towers City over seventy years ago and since then it had become the most recognizable landmark in Towers City with the Manicore dragon that sits atop their building; A two hundred and fifty ton statue of a rather imposing dragon of legend on a three hundred and seventy eight story tower.

On the street level of the plaza, there were a number of exclusive restaurants and stores. Places only the wealthy and privileged frequented and many of the unwashed would come and take pictures. There were also a number of street vendors present for those with more humble incomes.

During the week it was mostly a business atmosphere, but on the weekends the companies would shut down and street performers would come out and it would be like a weekly art fair in the middle of the plaza.

Jason was so mesmerized by everything he almost passed The Lauvre Cafe. He quickly locked his brakes and made a screeching noise as he stopped short. He got off the bike and walked over to the door. He examined the window and much to his relief, he saw a 'help wanted' sign sitting at the bottom of it. He quickly chained his bike to the stand outside and went in. He was surprised to note that it was practically empty. There were a few customers sipping from their cups. A few had laptops while the others watched the flat screen televisions that were anchored to the walls.

Jason walked up to the counter toward the back. As he got closer, the seductive aroma of coffee hit him. Suddenly a blonde, good looking guy with a goatee came running out from the kitchen with a phone wedged between his shoulder and ear.

"I know, Bethany!" He barked. "But I need money to run this dump! I don't care if you have to be someplace! This is a business and I can't pay the bills with your name! Bethany? Bethany!? Damn it!" He shouted as he threw his phone to the floor. Jason's eyes remained glued to him and as he turned to face Jason, his face broke into a nervous smile. "You saw that, didn't you?" Jason nodded. "Well, you try having Zsa Zsa for a sister and we'll see how well you do. Can I help you?" He asked.

"You're Tristan Lauvre,"

"Correct. Who are you?"

"I'm Jason Randwulf. I noticed you had a help wanted sign out front," Tristan made a pained look on his face.

"You saw that, did you?"

"You are looking for help, right?"

"Yes and no. I mean, I need help. No question, but I can't really afford anyone. At least, not full time."

"That's fine,"

"Really? I'm talking like ten hours a week. Maybe less. At minimum wage too."

"Oh." Jason said, trying to conceal his disappointment.

"But that's just until I can get my sister to release more money to me."

"How long will that take?"

"Hard to say. She kind of just lives in her little world." Tristan said. Jason looked around the place.

"Not to be rude, but I kind of expected this place to be busier,"

"You and me both. When Bethany and I first opened, it was packed. From open to close, it was wall to wall people, but I guess over time the novelty wore off. There's Coffee-Opolis up the street. They're the new it thing. You might be able to get something over there." he suggested.

"Thanks. I'll check them out." Jason said as he turned to leave.

"Wait!" Tristan yelped. Jason turned. "What about this place? I know there's not much to offer right now, but I really need help!

One man can't run all this seven days a week from morning 'til night! I'm going crazy! Please!"

"I don't know." Jason said and then Tristan leapt from behind the counter and grabbed Jason's legs.

"Please! I'm begging you! Save me!" Tristan whined. Jason looked down at him questioningly.

"Let me check some more places out and I'll get back to you," he said. Tristan jumped up and his face lightened.

"Okay!" He chirped. He then dashed back around to the counter and retrieved one of the business cards he had stacked next to the register. "Call me if you want the job," he said. His eyes were still begging as Jason stepped out.

Jason spent the rest of the day going in and out of coffee houses, cafes, and diners but no one was hiring. It seemed all the businesses in Towers City were doing too well, almost.

The sky was growing dark and the traffic was now clogged the other way towards the suburbs where everyone lived. Jason found himself cruising down the same street he had come in by and he stopped outside of the Lauvre Cafe. The events of the day played back in his head. Every polite nod and shook hand. All the managers telling him there was nothing currently, but if he would check back in a few months, there may be an opening. Jason got off his bike and chained it again. He walked into the cafe and it was even more empty than last time. The only customer was a rumpled looking old man whose attention was dedicated to the evening news that had just begun on the flat screen above him. Jason walked back to the counter and before he could make it, Tristan was on him.

"You're back!" he said with some surprise.

"Yeah. I guess you weren't aware that Coffee-Opolis isn't hiring now."

"I knew."

"What?"

"They haven't been hiring for months."

"Why didn't you tell me?"

"I just thought it would be good for you to see how busy they were. Maybe it would break your spirit enough to make this place look good." Jason fumed for a moment and then thought.

"You were right," he said at last. "No one seems to be hiring, so I guess it's you or nothing."

"Yes! You'd be surprised how many people choose nothing."

"I doubt that very much," Tristan was quick to whip out the papers Jason needed to sign to confirm his employment.

"Just fill these out and we'll get you started." Jason took the forms and a pen from next to the cash register and took a seat at a nearby booth. He was concentrating on the page before him when a very familiar voice came into earshot. He looked up and saw Tyler walking into the cafe, in uniform.

Jason felt his heart beat ten times faster than normal. Sweat was forming along his brow. He knew there was a chance of them running into each other sometime, but he didn't expect it so soon. He watched Tyler as he sauntered in and removed his hat. His hair was still that shade of brown he remembered. His face was handsome as ever, a bit older but it had been three years since they last laid eyes on each other. His voice was the same though. It was deep and soothing. It carried Jason away to a simpler time in Blue Haven.

Jason and Tyler had met in a history class during their first year at Blue Haven Community College. Jason had always been a poor student of history, but for Tyler, it came naturally. They spent many hours studying together in the library until one night, while studying for finals, they took a break and finally began talking to each other. Their conversation was meant only to be polite, but soon it began to reach much deeper levels. They were sharing private secrets neither had ever told anyone else and before they were done studying, they had shared their first kiss. The first of many.

Jason was so lost in his memory he hadn't noticed Tyler looking his way.

"Jason?" Tyler asked. Jason snapped back and saw Tyler approaching. "Jason Randwulf?"

"Tyler. Hi."

"I can't believe this. How are you? What are you doing here?"

"I'm fine and I'm actually getting a job here at the moment." Jason said and indicated to the forms he was working on.

"Oh. So, you moved here?"

"Yes. I got in just last night."

"You're kidding! This is incredible! Do you mind?" Tyler asked as he pointed to the seat across from Jason.

"Sure."

Tyler sat down quickly. His smile was radiant. The world began to close around them and they were back in their little bubble. Just the two of them.

"This is fantastic! I can't tell you how much I've missed you," Jason merely smiled.

"I missed you too."

"Dave is going to flip."

"Dave?"

"My boyfriend. Dave Fordham."

"You're seeing someone."

"Going on two years in June. We met during basic training and as luck would have it, they partnered us up," Tyler said. Suddenly the other officer that walked in with Tyler, the one Jason barely noticed, came walking up. He had a handsome face too. A little battle scarred and stubbly. A face with character. His body was thick, as evidenced by the way his uniform looked tight along his shoulders and chest.

"Who's this?" He asked in his deep, gravelly voice. Tyler slid over to make room for him.

"This is Jason Randwulf,"

"The Jason? Well, I've heard a lot about you." Dave said as he took Jason's hand into his. His hand was large and hairy and his grip was like a vice. "Nice to put a face with a name."

"So, Tyler's told you about me? Us?"

"Yeah, I know the whole story. What brings you to the big bad city?"

"Things were just getting stagnate back home and I figured it was time to strike out and find what I want to do with the rest of my life,"

"Cool. Thinking about joining the force? We can always use another good man."

"I don't think so. It's not really my thing. I just got a job here. We'll see where that gets me."

"Cool. We should be seeing you a lot then."

"Why?"

"Me and Ty come in here before our shifts every day. Pretty good coffee, but the best part is there's never any wait." Dave said and then gave a short, brusque laugh.

"Then, I guess I will see you guys around."

"We should let Jason get back to his paperwork," Tyler said. Dave then checked his watch.

"You're right. Roll in twenty. It was nice meeting you, Jay." Dave and Tyler then got up from their seats.

"Likewise, Dave." Jason said as he shook Dave's hand again. They turned from him and were heading for the door when Tyler turned around quickly.

"Hey! If you want, maybe we could all hang out sometime. We can show you the city and some of the clubs."

"Yeah! That would be fun! How 'bout it?" Dave asked.

"Sure. We can talk about it later."

"Great. My cell number's the same, so just give me a call," Jason nodded. Tyler and Dave then turned and walked out the door and disappeared around the corner.

5

The first month or employment at The Lauvre Cafe proved to be a sweet and sour experience for Jason. The hours left much to be desired and Tristan had a strange knack for scheduling him to come in just in time to see Tyler and Dave come in for their daily coffee fix. Tyler would sometimes ask about their tentative plans to hang out, but Jason simply sloughed it off and claimed he was too busy, but as soon as the craziness of his life died down, they would work something out.

The pay wasn't all that great either, as he only averaged about ten hours a week, and what few contacts and resources Jason had failed to find him anything better. The online ads had laundry lists of qualifications needed for even the most basic positions and usually at the top of those lists was experience. Experience that Jason did not possess.

The good part of the job was that he got a chance to soak up the energy of downtown. He saw a few local celebrities here and there, including Bethany Lauvre herself. He had only seen her on his little television, so when he saw her in person he was quite impressed. She really was very pretty with a fair complexion, silky blonde hair, a lilting voice, and a warm demeanor that really made you want to love her. Although, her spell over Jason was short lived as he saw her dark side as well. When she and Tristan went in back, she got down and dirty as they fought about how the cafe was to be run and how much money was really needed to maintain daily operations. Bethany seemed to have no patience for the business end of it, but preferred to be the face of the cafe while Tristan slaved countless hours to keep it afloat as best he could.

"I don't know what you do with the money I give you, but you are going to have to do a lot better than this!" She barked.

"For the bazillionth time, Beth," He started.

"It's Bethany! Bethany! Never Beth,"

"Fine, Bethany, I do the best I can with the little amount I have which I whimsically refer to as the profits! We do not have the business coming in that we need to keep this place open! Either we close, or you give me more money!"

"We are not closing!" she said with a stern look on her delicate face.

"Then write me a check." Tristan said flatly. He stormed past her and out to the front.

He looked around and saw only a little old lady reading a book as her little purse dog was on the floor drinking water from a little fur lined bowl and Jason dusting the tables. Bethany was close behind him.

"I can't afford to keep bailing you out," she said. He spun around to her.

"Bail me out? Let's not forget, sister dear, this all was your idea! You wanted a restaurant named after you. You wanted the notoriety of being a business owner. You wanted it all, and by God, you've got it!"

"And I hired you to manage it!"

"I need more money. Now, unless the next sentence out of your mouth is 'Of course, Tristan. Here's a check for a million dollars. Bye.' We have nothing more to discuss today," he said. Bethany locked her eyes on him and narrowed them, but unlike most other people she gave that look to, Tristan never backed down. She quickly grabbed her purse and, in an indignant march, stormed towards the door. She turned back to him as she held the front glass door open.

"I'll have a check sent out to you later," she said and hurried off in a huff.

Tristan sat down behind the counter as Jason walked up to him.

"Sounds like you two had quite a talk."

"Happens every couple weeks, but she'll write the check and I'll be able to keep this place open for another few months. It's the circle of life."

"A million dollars just keeps this place open for a few months?"

"Oh, she doesn't write a check for a million. I'll be lucky if I get fifty thousand out of her."

"She doesn't seem to be very interested in the success of the cafe."

"When she conned me into helping her open this place, she thought it would be so much more glamorous for her. She envisioned a place where she could put all the names of her enemies on a list and deny them access while letting in all her adoring fans and then she'd come in and they'd fawn all over her. The thing about my sister is that she is a bottomless pit of need and constantly seeks validation on nearly every level."

"But she's on TV. Everyone loves her."

"And that's not nearly enough for her. I don't think she'll be happy until the whole world worships at her altar."

"Wow."

"Exactly. Well, it's four. End of your shift. Thanks for coming in."

"Sure."

"Here's the schedule for next week." Tristan said as he handed Jason a sheet of paper. Jason quickly scanned it and gave a pained look.

"Five hours? That's it?"

"Sorry. Even if I get that check from Bethany, I'm still barely making it through this month. I'll keep working on her for some more, but until then, that's the best I can do."

"I understand. I guess I'll see you next week." Jason said and walked into the kitchen. There was no stove. Just a refrigerator where all the prepackaged food was kept chilled in case a customer was to order it.

Jason took off his apron and hung it on the hook next to the time clock, punched out and walked out the back door into the alley behind the cafe. He got his bike and pedaled back home.

Jason came skidding up to the stairs of the building and hoisted the bike over his shoulder and walked up. He checked the mail and then went on up to his apartment.

As he got to his door, Heather's opened and a couple screaming kids came running out and then down the stairs. Heather was close behind.

"Yours?" Jason asked.

"No. I babysit for some of the tenants."

"That's nice."

"I don't have anything better to do. I'm still living off a trust fund my grandmother set up for me. I figure I might as well do some good deeds in my spare time, right?"

"Sure," The kids came screaming back up to Heather. She grabbed them.

"Go on back and watch some TV. Aunt Heather needs to chat with her friend," she said to the kids. They quickly bolted into her apartment and shut the door behind them. She walked over to Jason just as he pushed his door open. "You want to talk about it?"

"Talk about what?"

"I'm sensing a lot of tension coming off of you," she said as she followed him inside.

"It's just been one of those days. I really don't want to talk about it."

"You know, normally I don't take such a personal interest in the folks who live here, but I've made an exception in your case. Don't make me regret that."

"It's just work. I can't get the hours I need to get a decent paycheck and I haven't been able to find anything better."

"There's more."

"There isn't. Really." Jason insisted. Suddenly, his cell phone rang. Jason tried to reach for it, but Heather was quicker and she snagged it. She checked the caller ID and it read Tyler Z. "Give it to me,"

"Who's Tyler?"

"No one. Give me my phone!" Heather quickly flipped it open and put it to her ear.

"Hello?" She asked as she dodged Jason's arms. "Hello, Tyler. My name's Heather. I'm a friend of Jason's. He's a little busy. I could take a message," Jason finally tackled Heather and managed his phone away from her.

"Hello, Tyler?" Jason asked. "No. She's just a friend. She's not good with boundaries. Yeah. I'm sorry, but it's been so nuts lately. I'm still not totally unpacked yet. Definitely. Yeah. You, me and Dave. Wouldn't miss it for the world. Bye." Jason then clicked off the phone.

"I ask again, who's Tyler?" Heather said smugly as she sat down on the couch.

"If you must know, he's my ex." Jason said.

"You're gay?"

"Is that a problem?"

"No. I just didn't realize. I don't really get that vibe off you."

"I've been meaning to get that fixed."

"And Tyler's your ex. Let me guess, Dave is not the name of his goldfish."

"No. His current."

"Ouch. You come all the way out here to reconnect with him, and he's taken."

"I did not come out here for Tyler."

"Yes, you did."

"No! I really didn't. Not totally."

"Ha! I knew it!"

"Okay. Maybe I had some ideas about getting back with him

in the back of my mind." Jason said as he joined Heather on the couch. "Then he walked in with Dave. He doesn't even look gay. He's so butch. He has no neck. The man has no neck at all!"

"Some people like that kind of thing."

"I guess."

"Ah, sweetie. It sucks, I know, but think about it. You have a whole city of new opportunities out there just waiting for you."

"That is if I can keep up with the rent. I'm okay with the money I have now, but when that runs out and I need this coffee shop job to sustain me, I'm dead." Jason lamented.

"I'd give you a break on the rent if it were up to me," Jason smiled at her.

"Thanks."

"Look, I better get back to the ankle biters. You'll be cool?"

"Yeah. I think I'm just going to try and relax. Come up with a plan."

"That's the spirit." Heather said as she shot up. "Never say die. By the way, I hope you don't mind, but I got your paper this morning and left it in the kitchen for you."

"I don't get the paper,"

"Well, today you do. Good night." Heather said as she zipped out the door.

After the sun went down and the early evening news was over, Jason heated up a frozen entree for dinner and after that he tried to relax with a hot shower. He emerged from the steamy bathroom in his robe and went straight to his bed.

He lied down on his back and his thoughts began to speed through his brain. He thought for a moment and got up again. He went to the kitchen and there was a Towers Tribune sitting on the counter, just as Heather said. Jason took the paper and brought it to his bed. He pulled the plastic cord off and unfolded it. He threw aside the front page and sports page. Tossed the travel and Metro sections. He finally found what he was looking for. The classified ads.

He flipped through page after page of the section. He found the help wanted ads and poured over them. Most of them read like scams and all the others were way beyond his skill set. He started checking some of the fringe categories in hopes of finding something unique yet profitable.

There were a few requests for artist models, females only. He then noticed an ad and he had to read it twice to make sure he was reading it correctly. It seemed to be asking for volunteers for some kind of scientific research. It was very vague and plain. The only part that really caught his eye was the promise of five hundred thousand dollars as compensation. He checked for any other ads like it, but there weren't any. He looked over the ad once more and then he noted the phone number. He knew it was probably a scam, but it seemed too good to just let it go. He grabbed his phone and dialed the number. A few rings and then a voice came on.

"You are calling about the ad?"

"Uh, yes,"

"Take this down. 2938 Industry Road. Unit 203. Be there tomorrow at ten in the morning." The voice said and the line went dead.

"Hello? Hello?" Jason asked. He quickly re-dialed but instead he got a message that the number had been disconnected. "Okay. It's probably a scam," He checked the time. It was a little past ten, but he was tired so he shut off the lights and slipped into bed.

As tired as he was, he couldn't get the phone call out of his mind. It seemed impossible anyone would offer so much money just to try a new diet pill or some new food additive. Either it was some deadly serious experiment that involved surgery or it was a scam and only one out of millions of volunteers would have a chance at the big money. He decided he wouldn't even bother with it, but as the night went on, he continued debating it.

By morning, Jason had gotten very little sleep and had finally decided that checking out the address wouldn't kill him. If it looked shady, he could just come back, no harm done. He had nothing better to do with his day anyway. He might even make a little money for his trouble. It was only eight, so he pulled out his map and checked the address, which he happened to remember, which he took as a sign of sorts, as he never could remember any address by heart. Not even his own.

He found the spot. It was far. Too far to bike so he decided calling a cab would be for the best. He got himself together and called for the cab.

It took a while for the driver to find the address, but he did find it. It was a rather run down looking area. Clearly, not a part of Towers City that was ever advertised. It was mostly comprised of old business complexes and small warehouses. A few places were still in business but mostly it was a place the homeless would gather to eat and sleep in peace. The building Jason was looking for stuck out a bit as it was the only building that had a fresh coat of paint on it. The windows in front had been blacked out and the address was barely legible from the street.

Jason got out of the car and told the driver to go on. He had no idea how long he would be and he could just call for a new cab later on his cell. The cab sped off back to the city as Jason approached the building. He was a few minutes early. He thought about waiting, but as he saw the local residents begin to shuffle around with their shopping carts, he felt it would be safer inside.

Jason walked in and was surprised. It looked so modern. The room was completely white. White floors, walls and ceiling and the furniture was white as well with some red accent pillows. A window in the wall opposite Jason opened and a young woman appeared. She had short hair and had a dazed smile on her face.

"Hello. How may I help you?" She asked. Jason stepped forward.

"I came about the ad."

"Of course," she held out a stack of forms to Jason. "Please fill these out and someone will be with you in a moment."

"I just wanted to know about the money. Are you really paying five hundred thousand dollars?" He asked. She stared back at him blankly.

"Fill out the forms and someone will be with you in a moment," she said again and then her window shut.

Jason took the forms and sat down on the couch. He then noticed the table in front of him. He set the forms down and then realized he had no pen. He got up and as he walked up to the small window, it opened again and the girl was still there smiling. Without a word, her arm shot out with a pen for him.

"Thanks," She then produced a glass of water.

"In case you get thirsty," she said.

"I'm fine. Thanks."

"Please. You will need to drink before we can conduct the test,"

"Look, if you could just tell me about the money,"

"Drink, please."

"Fine." Jason said as he took the glass from her. He sat back down and started filling out the forms. They went on forever. Each page seemed to ask the same questions as the previous page. He kept filling them out. As he did, he took sips from his glass. With the first sip, he noticed quickly that whatever it was, it wasn't water. It looked like water, but it tasted differently.

"Hey!" The window opened again. The girl looked at him.

"Yes?"

"This water tastes kind of funny,"

"Please just drink," she said and the window closed again. He got up and banged on it.

"Hey! Talk to me! What is this stuff? I have a right to know! I'm not your guinea pig yet!" He called out, but there was no answer. "The hell with this!" he said as he turned and headed for the door, but it was locked. He pulled at it harder but it wouldn't budge. He turned and he could see the room was filling with gas. He ran back to the window. "Hello! Is there anyone in there? There's some smoke out here! Hello?" He cried. He went for the door again, but his legs gave out under him and he fell to the floor. He soon began to go numb all over his body. He felt his eyes grow heavy and his head was spinning. He saw some figures crowd over him just before his eyes shut.

He suddenly felt awake, but there was only darkness around him. His arms felt pinned back and his legs were spread apart. He was starting to panic. It was as if he was floating in some kind of void as if in a dream. He heard loud noises, like drills, coming from nowhere. Suddenly, through the darkness, red began to bleed through. It didn't look like a liquid, but more like solid light. It slid through the inky darkness like blood through a series of veins. More drill noises and Jason felt a sharp pain in his wrists. He screamed out and the red that surrounded him surged. It drifted around him as if waiting to strike. He struggled to free his arms, but he was locked in his place. The red shot forward and engulfed him. He could feel it pushing against him all around. He felt it going into his ears and nose. His lungs were filling fast. He tried to scream but he couldn't get anything out. He felt a shock tear through him. His blood was on fire. The pressure was building in his body. He felt something trying to push through his flesh from the inside. Another jolt of pain swam through him and finally, he awoke.

5

Jason coughed violently as he woke up. He also noticed he was encased in some kind of body bag. His arms were throbbing with pain but his panic overrode any discomfort. He clawed quickly at the bag, trying to find a zipper or tear. He finally found a snag in the zipper and managed to open it up. He spilled out of it and tumbled from atop a pile of something to the floor. He quickly got his bearings. He looked around. He was in some kind of basement surrounded by large piles of bags similar to the one he just struggled out of. The only difference was that the other bags were full. He pressed down on one and it was clear it had a body inside. There had to be thousands stacked from one end of the cavernous basement to the other. The only light available flickered like fire. He peered around and saw a huge furnace not too far away. Some figures clothed in what looked like some sort of bio hazard suits were milling around.

He couldn't hear what they were saying, but he could see a few more a few yards away who were piling the body bags onto a cart. After the cart was full, they took it over to the furnace and dumped the bags inside. The flames roared and the light grew brighter. Jason shrunk back and crawled along to the back wall. He then noticed he was only wearing a shirt and his boxer shorts. He didn't know what to do. If he announced his presence, he didn't see much hope in being allowed to go, but he also didn't want to get ashed.

He turned and noticed the outline of a door. He felt along the wall and it was indeed a door. Rusted over after years of neglect, but a door nonetheless. He pushed on it slightly and it gave a bit to his weight. He could hear the suited figures loading more corpses onto their cart. They were closer. He pushed on the door harder. He could feel the air outside seep in. He gave one last push and it burst open. Behind him, there was an avalanche of dead bodies that covered his escape. He ran. He didn't think about anything else. He just ran as fast as he could in any direction.

Jason had been running through the streets of Towers in his underwear for what seemed like hours. He stopped finally and rested in a small alley. It was night. His feet were sore and blistered and he had no idea where he was exactly. It was night and the streets seemed to be relatively empty so it had to be late. He hadn't detected any voices behind him so he was pretty sure no one had followed him so he continued on his way at a leisurely walk.

He finally made it back to familiar ground at long last. The streets were barren so he was able to navigate through them safely. He was so close to home. It was only a block away. He found the alley that cut through to the back of his building. It was dark, but he really didn't care. The sooner he got home, the better he thought.

He started down but halfway there, he saw three figures run into the alley. He stopped and hid behind some trash cans. He looked over and saw that the figures were men. The two larger ones seemed to be victimizing the smaller third.

"Please! I don't want any trouble. I was just walking home." The small one said. His voice was drenched with fear.

"We saw you holding hands with that other fag." One of the larger men said. He pushed the little guy against the wall. "You know, it's just so gross!"

"We weren't hurting anyone!"

"You were hurting the fabric that we have built our society on."

The other large one said. It sounded like he had some college under his belt as he spoke in a controlled tone and with some degree of education. "You and people like you are tearing this country apart by perverting the most sacred foundation of our society."

Jason ducked back into the shadow. He could hear the two large guys lay into the little guy. He cried out with each blow. He then heard a metallic noise, like a switchblade being unsheathed. Then Jason felt a sharp pain in the back of his neck, like a spider bite, but then he felt something enter him. He looked down and a black liquid began ooze out of his pores. He almost screamed, but a blanket of fluid wrapped around his face and formed a mask over his whole head.

Soon, the fluid was all over his body. He fell to the ground and tried to pull it off, but it was like it fused to his skin. Then suddenly, a feeling of euphoria struck him. Something else had taken control of his brain. He stood up and walked toward the three men.

The little guy was too scared to speak as one of his tormentors was threatening him with a knife. His friend noticed Jason approaching.

"What in the hell are you?" he said. Jason looked down at a puddle on the ground. He saw himself, but it wasn't him. He was clothed in a black suit with three V shaped lines over his chest. Weird red symbols were scrawled along his arm and neck and his eyes glowed with blue light. He looked over at the two bullies and he raised his arm. A blast of white energy surged from the palm of his hand and sent one of the toughs flying. The one with the blade came charging but Jason fired a bolt of energy which caught the knife. He was able to then pull the knife from the guy's hand and redirect it into his leg.

The punk howled in pain as the knife lodged deep into his leg. He fell back, clutching his wounded limb. His friend was back up and advancing quickly. He threw a punch, but Jason caught it easily and then shot out his fist and hit the guy right in his stomach. He fell back in pain. Jason pushed him back and he fell on top of his friend.

"Go." Jason said, but his voice was bigger. Like some kind of monster or something. They both struggled up and hurried away as best they could, screaming all the way. Jason turned his attention to their victim. He was bloodied up some, but no major damage had been done, it seemed. He'd have a black eye for a few weeks, but he was alive. He was backed against the wall and shivering in fear.

"Who are you?" Jason did not know how to respond.

"A friend," he said simply. Jason took a step forward, but the guy tore off in the opposite direction.

Jason looked around and wasn't sure what was happening. Suddenly, he felt a surge of energy surrounding him. Light filled his vision and he was becoming lighter. Before he knew it, he was flying up to the roof of his building. He found his skylight and drifted in. As he landed, everything metal in the apartment shook violently and with a surge, the light he was radiating died. Jason caught his reflection in a mirror quickly and he got a better look at his appearance. Whatever he was wearing accented his natural musculature and seemed to form a new body over his old one. He touched his chest and it felt like it was his skin, only under a thin layer of slime.

"What is this?" He asked to himself. He suddenly felt whatever enter him leave. The suit receded back into his body and Jason fell over onto his bed, where he then passed out.

Police sirens woke Jason up. He struggled out of bed and looked out the window. He saw two cop cars sitting on the corner with the guy he saved talking to them. Jason suddenly felt the memories of the previous night race back to him. He quickly dressed and dashed downstairs.

Jason ran to the street and saw the police were still there. He saw Heather nearby.

"What's going on?"

"Some poor guy got bashed last night. The police said two pin heads chased him down and beat him up just because they caught him holding hands with his boyfriend."

"Is he okay?"

"He looks like he'll live. I guess he's telling them some weird guy in tights saved him."

"They told you all of this?"

"No, I just overheard. I come from a long line of snoops," she said. Jason walked over and as he did, he could recognize Tyler as one of the cops talking with the victim. It looked as though they were finishing up, so Jason hurried over.

"Hey," he said. Tyler looked up and smiled.

"Jason. What are you doing here?" Jason pointed to the building.

"Live here. What's going on?"

"Nothing. I mean, something. This guy got bashed last night in this alley. He brought us here to see if we could find some evidence of who his attackers were."

"Is that all he said?"

"That's all he told me that I'm putting in the report." Tyler said as he closed his notepad.

"There was more?"

"Yeah, but it's crazy." Tyler said with a laugh. He looked around. He saw Dave in the alley checking for any fluids such as blood or sweat. Tyler leaned closer to Jason. "I shouldn't tell you." He whispered. "But, the guy says some dude in tights saved him."

"What?"

"I know. Crazy. He says the guy shot some kind of energy out of his hands and chased them off."

"Wow. Are you sure he's making it up?"

"Of course. He had been out drinking with his boyfriend, and frankly just by looking at him, I'm sure that's not all he'd been doing. He probably was just on a bad trip."

"But something chased those bashers away."

"Could have been a police car passing by. A cat knocking over a trash can. Anything, but I really doubt it was some energy shooting super freak."

"Still, it sucks. I'd think stuff like this would be beyond Towers

City. At least, from what I've heard."

"In general, yes. Towers is a very liberal, progressive place, but no matter where you go you're always going to find that fringe of haters. It happens way too often to suit me, I'll tell you that much."

"Jay!" Dave called as he came running up from behind.

"Dave. Hi."

"Tyler filling you in, huh?"

"Yeah. I can't believe this happened. I mean, I live right up there and I didn't hear a thing."

"Are you sure? If you heard anything, no matter how insignificant it may seem, it would really help." Tyler urged.

"I'm sure. Sorry."

"Oh well. I think I got some blood anyway. Another one for the books. Hey! Now that we're all together, maybe we can talk about getting together!" Dave said excitedly. Tyler's expression lit up quickly.

"Yeah! How about tomorrow night?" Tyler asked directing his eyes to Jason. Jason's heart stopped. He looked around and saw no escape. There was no real excuse available to him.

"I have to work." Jason said.

"Yeah, but the cafe closes at nine. We wouldn't even be heading out until eleven. You'd have plenty of time." Dave said. Jason's brain raced for another excuse, no matter how feeble, but he failed.

"Then I guess tomorrow is fine," he said with a half smile.

"Great!" Tyler said. "We'll swing by here to pick you up about eleven thirty. Cool?"

"Sure. I'm in 302."

"Perfect. We'll see you tomorrow night, then."

"Can't wait," He watched as Tyler and Dave helped their victim into the car and then got in themselves. Jason really noticed how well Tyler moved in his uniform. Very graceful and free, despite the bulky belt slung around his waist. He dipped into the driver's seat next to Dave and the car lit up as he turned the key. It eased forward and up the street and soon was out of sight.

6

Jason did everything he could to prolong his work day, but it was of no use. Tristan had him come in for only three hours and was firm that there was no over time he could have. Jason got on his bike and started on his way home. All the way, he was dreading the night that lay ahead.

It was bad enough just to see Tyler and Dave together, but to be forced to spend the entire evening watching them in couple mode did not entice him. It was so bad, it even managed to eclipse his memories of weirdness about the evening prior. He had barely given the black liquid a single thought. He didn't really have reason to.

As the day went on, he felt nothing different. He had rested and there were no signs of anything wrong. No headache. No fatigue. No black liquid shooting out of his skin involuntarily. Perhaps, he thought for a moment, the whole thing just had been a nightmare of some sort. Images of some old comic book he had read years ago coming up for no apparent reason. He stopped in front of his building and looked down at his arm. He gave it a sharp poke, but nothing happened. He accepted that as a sign he was cured and carried his bike on up to his unit.

He shut the door and took in his apartment. It was completely squared away, save for a handful of boxes stacked in the corner. His books were set on their shelves. His clothes were crammed as best they could be in his closet. A month in Towers City and things finally started to reach some level of normalcy. He checked the clock on the wall. It was barely three in the afternoon and Dave and Tyler weren't due to come by until eleven. He thought hard about everything he could do but nothing really interested him. Nothing could cheer him up enough to forget the prospect of seeing Tyler in the arms of another man. Jason then opted instead to lie down on the bed. He wasn't tired, exactly, but he couldn't think of anything better to do. He lied on his back, staring at the ceiling. The shadows crawled along as the hours did.

Soon, his eyes grew heavy and he fell asleep. There was only darkness in his vision, but soon he began to hear things. It wasn't abnormal for Jason to hear things in his dreams. He had audio in them and he dreamt in color as well. He always took pride in that since he had been told that dreaming in color was a sign of intelligence. He just assumed audio dreaming was an even greater sign of intelligence. It was different though. What he was hearing was far more clear and a lot louder than normal. It started as low chanting, then a rumbling started. Soon, the sound of clanging was heard. The din of a metal on metal choir. All the noises quickly mingled together and it was sounding more like a battle. A war. Screams and cries of blood howled in his ears and soon the visions came.

He saw great fields that spanned across what had to have been millions of miles far and wide, and upon those fields was a sea of bloodied bodies, writhing and fighting each other. Swords of spectacular size and design shining in the light of three suns. Enormous beasts of indescribable power and strength trudging through the bodies below them, roaring in great rage. The distinct sound of flesh being pierced soon added to the cacophony.

Soon, Jason realized he wasn't dreaming, because he soon realized he was no longer asleep. He was still on his bed, but somehow he was awake and seeing something real right before him. The carnage was unlike anything he could have imagined. Millions of men and women clashing swords, axes and all other manner of weapons. Blood seeping beneath them and staining the green ground below them with crimson.

As the scene played out, Jason began to feel something. A sense of guilt. He couldn't imagine why, but some part of him grew anxious and sad, as if he had put the war into action himself. A great and deep remorse overcame him as he saw more bodies fall lifeless below him. The pain of each loss stabbed at him like a dagger in his heart. The pain grew more powerful until he could take no more. He let out a great scream and then his vision filled with white light and just as quickly as that, he was back in his apartment, on his bed. Bolt upright. He looked over and saw it was well past ten at night. He was covered in sweat and his body was trembling. He did his best to regain his composure and soon his mind caught up with him. Tyler and Dave would be there soon.

He got up and went straight for the bathroom. He stripped and got into the shower. The warm water poured over him and it relaxed his body. He took the soap and lathered it all over himself. He was still thinking about his dream, but as best he could, he couldn't recall any clear image. He found it odd since he remembered how clear and real everything seemed. It was as though a part of his brain was intentionally blocking his recollections. He disregarded it all and then poured a bit of shampoo into his hair. He massaged it in and looked down. He saw a trace of black liquid in the water at his feet. Soon he saw another and then another. He looked at his hands and saw copious amounts of black liquid on them. He shifted into panic and stuck his head directly under the stream of water. Black came pouring down from his head and soon the tub was covered. His breath began to grow short. He reached for the door of the shower, but suddenly the blackness shifted and shot back up at him. It swirled around him and was all over his skin. He clawed away at it, but it soon soaked back into his body. Jason leaned back against the wall, his limbs growing numb, and reexamined himself. He rinsed quickly and got out of the shower. He went to the mirror and leaned in as close as he could to get a better look.

"What the hell is going on?" He asked himself. A knock at the door broke his thoughts.

"Hello?" Tyler called out.

"Hey, guys!" Jason answered. "I'll be out in a second!"

Jason quickly ran out of the bathroom and dressed. He just threw on whatever he could grab and in record time, he was dressed and ready. He pulled the door open and saw Tyler and Dave standing together, arm in arm.

"You fall in?" Dave asked with a sharp laugh. Jason smiled.

"Sorry. I lost track of time. Let's hit it," he said in as happy a tone as he could muster.

Dave and Tyler took Jason downtown to a club known only as Skye. They told him it was the hottest club in town and in a town like Towers, that was saying something. It was a mixed gender club, but the majority of the patrons were gay men and that fact was not lost on the owner of Skye. They made sure it was a welcoming environment for all people from all walks of life. Money was money.

There were lots of ornate lighting devices including neon sculptures on the walls and disco balls at nearly every corner of the dance floor. As they walked in, Jason was blown away by all the activity. The dance floor was packed and the circular bar in the center had at least three layers of bodies in front of it. The music was loud and pounding as the lights danced along the walls. The dance floor was fairly well lit, but other than that, it was a rather dimly lit establishment. Bodies just kept coming at Jason from front to back and side to side. He slid through the tight mesh of people, following closely behind Tyler and Dave. They finally made it to the other side of the bar and found a clear spot to stand.

"I'll go get the drinks." Dave volunteered and then looked over at Jason.

"Just a beer," he said. Dave smiled and looked to Tyler.

"Get three of the usual,"

"You got it. I'll be right back." Dave said and disappeared into the crowd.

It was a particularly busy evening at Skye. Jason had seen movies with scenes that took place in clubs like Skye, but he never really understood what it was like to be in amongst all those people.

"A long way from Blue Haven, huh?" Tyler asked.

"You can say that again. This is incredible. You guys come here a lot?"

"When we can. Work keeps us pretty busy."

"I'll just bet." Jason said as he looked out to the sea of bodies surrounding them. "You guys really expect me to meet someone in all of this?"

"Well, we know it's not that cut and dry. We just thought since you're new in town, we'd help you get into the social scene."

"You two met in the police academy. How do you even know what the 'social scene' here is?"

"It's true we met during training, but not on campus. I snuck out and came here one night and this is where I ran into Dave. That's how I figured out his little secret."

"I was going to say. He doesn't really register on my gaydar."

"He's definitely one of a kind." Tyler said with a smile. The music got louder and neither Jason nor Tyler could continue the conversation.

"So, we're just not going to talk about it,"

"About what?"

"Us."

"There is no us, Jason. That was a long time ago."

"I realize that, but it did happen. It just would have been nice to have a little closure. You just said you wanted something more in life and then took off."

"Was there more I had to say?"

"How about good bye?"

"I said good bye."

"In a note. You never even called."

"You never called me."

"I'm not the one who left. You left me. I think the responsibility of calling falls to the one who left. I had enough to deal with."

"Now is really not a good time to talk."

"Then when would be?" Jason asked. Tyler's eyes locked onto Jason's but before he could say anything, Dave's voice broke the moment.

"Three usuals!" he said as he pushed three bottles in between Tyler and Jason. They each took one. Dave held his bottle up over his head and looked to Jason.

"To new friends," he said. Tyler raised his and looked to Jason again.

"To old friends."

"Bottoms up," Jason said. They clinked their bottles together and drank. Jason was impressed. He had never been a real beer drinker, but he had to note that whatever Dave had ordered was pretty good.

The night seemed to drag on for Jason. He was feeling too self-conscious to really try and connect with anyone and Dave and Tyler were always running on and off the dance floor as the songs changed.

It was about the time when everyone who had coupled up, were deeply entrenched with their mates. Jason was sitting at the bar nursing his fourth beer. He was looking into the crowd on the dance floor. He saw Tyler dancing with Dave. He had a big smile on his face as his body slid and slinked to the beat of the music. The lights flashed red and blue and then green and yellow at a hypnotic pace. He then saw Dave's arm hook around Tyler's waist and he pulled him in tight. Jason felt a slight fire burn in his stomach and was quick to put it out with another sip of beer.

"Jason?" A familiar voice asked. Jason turned and saw Heather walking toward him.

"Heather. What are you doing here?"

"It's Friday night. I have no life. Where else would I be? You?"

"Out with the ex," he said and pointed to Tyler and Dave.

"Which one?"

"The one with the lighter hair."

"Wow. Cute."

"Thanks."

"Not to rub it in or anything."

"It's okay. It sucks trying to be friends with an ex."

"Why'd you break up?"

"We knew each other in Blue Haven. He decided to do something with his life and I chose the opposite. That was about six years ago and now he's a fine, upstanding member of Towers City's finest, with a loving boyfriend, and I am practically unemployed with absolutely zero on the horizon."

"Whoa. Bitter much?"

"Sorry. It's been one of those weeks. And I'm topping the whole thing off with a fun filled night out with them."

"Sounds pretty screwed up to me."

"It is, but lately, my whole life has been going the way of screwed up."

"You really need to start being more positive. You can't spend the rest of your life beating yourself up just because things didn't go according to your plan. I believe that everything happens for a reason, and right now, you are where you need to be."

"In a bar?"

"You know what I mean. The gears of fate and destiny have brought you to this place for a reason and it's only a matter of time until you figure out what that reason is." Heather said.

"You forgot 'the force is strong in this one.'"

"Make fun if you want, but that's what I believe. There's a greater good out there we all serve, in our own ways, but you'll never figure out what it is if you keep wallowing in self-pity!" Jason regarded her carefully.

"You're right. I'm sorry," he said with a slight bow of his head.

"How many of those have you put away?"

"Enough. Enough to almost forget where I am and what I'm

doing." Jason said as Tyler and Dave returned as the last song began to end.

"Hey, who's this?" Dave asked as his eyes found Heather.

"Heather Rhett. I live across from Jason here,"

"Oh. Nice to meet you," Tyler said.

"Likewise. I was just chatting with Jay here and he says he's about ready to go."

"It's not even one yet." Dave protested. "This party hasn't even started yet."

"It's okay. I can take him. No reason for you two to cut it short." Heather said and placed her arm over Jason's shoulder.

"I don't know. Jason?" Tyler asked. Jason looked up at him with his bleary eyes. He then looked to Heather, and then back to Tyler and Dave.

"Yeah, I think I'm about partied out. Thanks though. It's been a lot of fun,"

"Yeah. We gotta do this again!" Dave said. Jason merely nodded to his suggestion. Heather helped him off his stool and he hugged them both, and then she maneuvered Jason through the crowd as best she could toward the door.

As they pushed through and got out to the street, Heather hooked her arm around Jason's and led him toward her car.

"Like I said. Everything happens for a reason," she said smugly. Jason leaned his head onto her shoulder and they continued on.

7

Jason and Heather walked into the brownstone and she quickly noticed Jason's mood had not lifted since they had left the club.

"You okay?" She asked as they climbed the stairs.

"I don't know. I guess." Jason said with his head pointing to his chest. He moved up the stairs slowly, as though his clothes weighed a couple of tons.

"So, the answer would be 'no'."

"Yes."

"You're really hung up on this guy, aren't you?"

"He was my first love. You don't really ever get over that."

"Sure you do."

"How can you say that? Have you ever gotten over whoever your first love was?"

"My first love is science, and that never leaves us."

"Fine. Cute. I'm talking about people here! Emotions! When Tyler and I met, we were just a couple of hormone crazed teens, but we connected. We became friends, and as the years passed and we discovered things about each other, we supported one another. He was the first person who really knew me. He knew who I was. He loved me for that and I loved him. We came out together. We..." Jason stopped suddenly as something caught in his throat. He turned from Heather quickly.

"I'm sorry."

"It's fine. I'm fine." Jason said as he straightened up.

"I have some coffee. If you want to talk."

"I think I'd like the coffee. Not the talk."

"Understood."

Heather led Jason up to her door and quickly opened it up. They walked in and as Heather went straight for her kitchen, Jason was glued to the floor as he looked around. He saw rather large and advanced computer equipment strewn from one end of the living room to the other. Monitors and lights were beeping and flashing left and right. It was less an apartment and more of a research facility. He looked down and was comforted to see a sofa in the middle of the room with a large coffee table in front of it. He sat down, his eyes still studying the unique decor of Heather's place.

"I'm a little bit of a science nut," she said as she hurried in with two cups of steaming coffee. She handed one to Jason and sat next to him on the couch. "I hope you can stand instant," she said.

"It's fine. Thanks." Jason said as he sipped from his cup.

"I know what you're thinking."

"No. No, you don't."

"My dad works for Manicore in their research department and he gives me first dibs on their rejected or outdated equipment. Most of this stuff doesn't even work, but I like to tinker," she said.

"What do you do with all this stuff?"

"Nothing much. I just like to have a project."

"I don't get this. I thought you were a trust fund baby."

"I am, but I went to school before that. I graduated from MIT a couple years after high school, then I got a degree from Oxford. I did a one year internship with NASA...."

"Whoa! MIT? NASA? Are you some kind of genius?"

"Just a minor one."

"So, with all this brain power, you just hang out here fixing machines and babysitting children?"

"We all take our own paths." Heather said.

"But you could be..."

"Just another research drone like a million other geniuses out there. I've been under a microscope since I was eight, when my father discovered I was gifted, and I got sick of it. All I've ever wanted was to be free to do what I want. Whatever that might entail. Some days I like to dissect atoms with a particle accelerator, other days I like to paint, or make some pottery or something. I just wanted the freedom to choose."

"Sounds reasonable."

"Tell my dad. He says he gets me this stuff to encourage me, but I know he's just hoping to lure me into his footsteps."

"Would it be so bad? He makes good money, right?"

"Sure, but that's not what I'm about. I have money. I just want to hold onto who I am, and a job like that, with a company like Manicore, just sucks away your soul. That I won't give up."

"You're very odd."

"I know, but what fun is life if you're normal?"

"Granted. Look, thanks for the coffee, but I think the best thing for me now is to just get to bed."

"All right. My door's always open if you do want to talk."

"I'll keep that in mind. Again, thanks for the coffee." Jason said as he set his cup down and headed for the door.

Jason returned to his apartment and quickly stripped and fell into his bed, not even bothering to turn on a single light. He pulled the sheet over his head in some infantile attempt to shield his brain from his thoughts. He tried as best he could to keep from rehashing the evening to no avail. He couldn't help but replay his night in his head, step by step. All the emotions that flooded through him earlier came rolling back, like an Earthquake. His mind stuck on the image of Tyler and Dave dancing together at the club. Dave's hands on Tyler's arms. The smile on Tyler's face as he looked into Dave's eyes. Jason shut his eyes tighter and tried even harder to will himself to sleep.

Hours went by and Jason finally succumbed to his fatigue. His mind drifted away from the pain he was feeling and he passed on to other dreams. Visions began to swirl in his brain when he felt a familiar sensation overcome him. A cool, piercing sensation at the base of his neck. His eyes fluttered quickly, but he fell back into his deep slumber. He began to see new images form. Brilliant, bright images. He saw a large, green field surrounded by mountains and rocks. A bright sapphire sky above and then suddenly millions of tiny figures roaring onto the field. One hoard of screaming people rushing out and clashing with an opposing crowd coming from the other side of the field. The sound of screaming filled the air. Jason could hear the distinct chime of metal swords locking. It was war. A great and violent war.

Jason's vision came closer and he could see more closely as both armies continued to fight. The soldiers seemed to be outfitted with swords and shields and other types of medieval weapons. Grunts and cries of pain were coming from all around. Blood ran along the ground like water. Orders were being called out and as they were, more waves of soldiers pushed forward and the sounds of bodies being hit and bones being broken echoed out like a chorus.

Suddenly the sky went from blue to blood red. Black clouds framed the hellish sky above and the war showed no signs of ending. Warrior after warrior fell to the ground. The soil beneath was so wet with blood, it was like mud. Soon, there were only two lone fighters standing. The last of each side. A feeling of guilt suddenly overcame Jason. A guilt he had never felt before. It was so deep and real, he could almost feel himself about to cry. The two warriors stood among the bodies of their fallen brethren. One was tall with long hair and held a large axe. His armor was cracked and stained with blood and gore. There was a deep cut along his forearm covered in dried blood. The other was lean. His armor had been worn away completely and stood with his broad sword held ready. His left arm, however, was covered in some kind of black substance. It wasn't a fluid of any kind, because it had formed around his arm perfectly, like a second skin. Jason's vision diverted to his own body, and he realized he was also covered in the same way. The suit had formed around his body completely. He looked up quickly and saw the two warriors lunge at each other with their weapons with a final battle cry, and just as their weapons ripped into each other, Jason was pulled back.

Jason jumped up from his pillow, soaked with sweat. He looked around. It was still dark. He reached to the back of his neck but discovered nothing. He got up and padded to the bathroom. He switched on the light and looked into the mirror. His skin was shiny and weird. He touched his face and was surprised to find his skin was cold as ice. He slumped forward and soon his brain caught up with him. He turned to the shower and started the hot water. He watched intently as the water shot out of the shower head. He took off the rest of his clothes and as he stepped into the water stream, he felt the water warm his body. The water began to get hotter, but he just let it wash over him. He could see his skin growing red. The sting of the heat was nagging at him, but he refused to move.

"Get out of me," he said under his breath. He turned up the hot water. It was like lava pouring over him. His skin was growing even more red. A blister was beginning to form on his arm when he relented at last and jumped out. He slipped on the tiles and fell hard on the floor. He was paralyzed in pain but soon it soothed. The air on his skin was torture but it soon stopped. He saw the redness of his skin fade. He began to laugh all of a sudden. He slowly shifted his torso around and got to his feet. His body felt empty and weak. He trudged back to his bed and fell down on it. He pulled the sheet over him again and he quickly fell back to sleep.

8

The rain had begun earlier in the morning and it had been pouring all day. Jason was drenched when he walked into the cafe for his two hour afternoon shift. He wheeled his bike through the doors but Tristan was quick to speak.

"Jason, you can't bring that thing through here! Park it in the alley in back."

"That's what I was doing, but if it's all right with you, I'm wet enough already. I just wanted to cut through here, where it's dry."

"I get that, but you're tracking dirt in." Tristan whined.

"I'll clean it up. Don't worry," Jason said. His aggravation was difficult to disguise. He hadn't been getting much sleep over the past few days and his evening out with Tyler and Dave still clung to his thoughts like an irritating leech. He pushed past Tristan, through the kitchen and out to the alley where he secured his bike to the rack. He went back in and put on his apron and then gave himself a quick once over in the mirror. His damp hair was hanging down over his face and his clothes seemed rumpled and baggy. Jason slicked his hair back and readjusted himself as he walked back out to clean up the trail of wet dirt his bike had left behind.

"Are you okay, Jason?"

"I'm fine." Jason replied as he got on his knees and started wiping up the mess.

"I just ask because lately you've seemed a little on edge."

"I guess I've just not been in the best of moods lately."

"Any reason why?"

"Of course there's a reason," Tristan waited a moment for more, but Jason just kept to his task.

"And what is the reason?"

"I really don't want to talk about it. If it's fine with you, I just want to work." Jason said, his attention primarily on the floor.

"Whatever you say."

There were even fewer customers that day as the rain was doing a good job of keeping people indoors. There was only a lone customer sitting at the counter, sipping a cup of coffee. He was intent on the television above and Tristan was in back going over the books. Jason was making his third sweep around the tables when he noticed it was only a half hour until his shift was over. He sat down at one of the booths and looked out onto the street. The water was coming down in sheets and the street was barely visible under all the pounding splashes of the droplets. He became more aware of how the bad weather was only feeding his dark mood. Tristan suddenly came out from the kitchen, holding a slip of paper. He walked over to Jason and handed it to him.

"What's this?"

"New schedule for next week. Sorry." Tristan said. Jason scanned it quickly and looked back up at Tristan.

"You have got to be kidding me!"

"I'm sorry! I wish I had the money to get you in here more, but it's tight right now. I'm lucky I can still afford to keep this place open."

"I know, but this is worse than this week! I can't live on this!"

"My hands are tied. Look, it's dead here. Why don't you take off now? I'll credit you for the full hour."

"Thanks." Jason said as he stuffed his schedule into his pocket.

As Jason cruised down the street, the rain began to come down harder. He could feel the back of his shirt getting soaked and the water running down his back as he pumped harder. Fortunately there wasn't much traffic and once he turned on Park Street, there wasn't any at all. He kept an easy pace through the pouring rain when he suddenly heard his phone ring. He slid to a stop on the side of the road and ran over to a hanging awning over a nearby store. Once he was out of the downpour, he clicked his phone on.

"Hello?"

"Good afternoon. May I speak with Jason Randwulf?"

"Speaking."

"Mr. Randwulf. This is Premier National Bank. We are calling to inform you that a check in the amount of six hundred dollars has been cited for insufficient funds."

"Excuse me? What?"

"We realize you value your credit rating and we're sure you are anxious to rectify this issue as soon as possible."

"Wait. No, this is impossible. That was my rent check. It was good."

"Not according to our records, Mr. Randwulf. A deposit of at least six hundred dollars will be required in the next forty eight hours in order to bring your account current. Thank you for your time." Jason clicked off his phone and squeezed it hard in frustration. He stomped toward his bike and as he was about to push off, the chain snapped and he fell forward onto the wet ground. As Jason got up from under the bike, he grabbed the chain and quickly inspected it. His phone rang again.

"Yes?"

"Jason?"

"Mom! Hi. How are you?"

"I'm fine, sweetie. How are you?"

"I'm great."

"You don't sound great."

"I'm fine. Really. What is it?"

"Nothing. Just calling to see how things were going. We haven't heard from you in a while."

"I'm sorry. It's just been crazy with moving and finding a job."

"How's the new apartment?"

"It's nice. I mean, I have a few more things to get straightened out, but other than that, it's a dream."

"Good. Did you call Tyler?"

"Yes. We talked."

"I'm glad. I'd hate to think of you all alone in that city."

"I'm fine there. I live across the hall from my apartment manager and she's actually pretty cool."

"She? Oh."

"Don't go there, mom."

"I didn't say anything. I just think it's nice there's a nice girl nearby."

"Uh-huh. Look, I gotta get going. I'll call you later."

"Okay. We love you."

"Love you too. Bye." Jason said and clicked off his phone again. He got up from the ground and pulled the bike up. He slung the chain over his shoulder and continued home on foot. He made it two blocks before a police car came sliding up behind him. He turned and he could see Tyler behind the wheel. He knew it was a moment that could not be escaped, so Jason stopped and waited for the inevitable. The car came to a stop and the window slid down.

"Tyler. Hi."

"Hi. I thought that was you. I tried the cafe but Tristan said you had left. I was looking for you."

"You were?" Jason said as he stepped closer to the car.

"Yeah. I haven't heard from you since we all went out. I just wanted to know if you were all right."

"I'm fine."

"Really? You seemed kind of upset when you left."

"Maybe that's because I was."

"Why? I thought you were having fun."

"I wasn't. I lied. I was having a terrible time."

"Why didn't you say something?"

"Because if I had, you two would have just suggested that we go somewhere else or do something else, and that would have been worse."

"How would that be worse?"

"Because I was out with you! You and your new boyfriend." Jason barked. Tyler turned away slightly. "I know when you guys came by I was cool and happy with it all, but I'm not! Is it really any surprise to you that I may not have been comfortable going out with you and Dave?"

"I just thought we were past all of this. What we had was great, but that was a long time ago."

"I know it was a long time ago! I realize that! It doesn't make it any easier to see you with someone else. Watching you two dance close together. Touching. All the while, knowing how it was when it was you and me touching. How it felt. Maybe it's petty or small, but it just makes me mad thinking about it. Seeing it just makes it worse."

"I'm sorry. I guess it was a mistake."

"It's just something I need to get over. I know this. I want to be friends with you guys. I do, but it's going to take some time."

"I understand."

"Good." Jason said as he took his bike and continued walking away. Tyler pulled up to Jason again quickly.

"You need a ride?"

"I'm fine,"

"It's raining really hard. I can give you a lift."

"It's not that bad." Jason said as a crash of thunder blasted across the sky. The rain began to increase in intensity. Tyler pushed a button in the car and the backseat opened up.

"Toss the bike in. I'm taking you home," Jason couldn't find an argument, so he slid the bike into the car and sat up front next to Tyler.

The car started up the street smoothly. Jason tried to avoid looking at Tyler. There was no sound between them except for the car's radio that intermittently called out codes and police calls from around the city.

"Up here. Right." Jason said under his breath. Tyler steered the car around the corner smoothly and Jason could see the brownstone at the end of the block. Halfway there, Jason looked up at Tyler.

"Right here's fine," he said. Tyler parked the car easily and opened the rear doors. "Thanks," Jason said.

"You're welcome. Anytime," Jason smiled weakly and quickly got out. He pulled the bike out and closed the door after and then hurried home. Jason watched Tyler drive away from the steps of his building.

As he walked inside, the rain began to ease down to a mere drizzle. Jason, in frustration, threw his broken bike to the floor and stomped up the stairs to his apartment. As he walked to his door, he could hear the TV blaring in Heather's place, but he had no intention of knocking. He just pushed his door open and threw it shut quickly. He hurried to his closet and pulled out some clean, dry clothes and quickly changed.

He sat down on the couch and flicked the TV on with every intention of losing himself in some mindless diversion. Just as he found something, there was a knock on his door.

"Yes?"

"Company?" Heather called from the other side. Jason rolled his eyes.

"Sure," The door opened and Heather scampered in, settling on the other end of the couch. She sat there looking at him carefully.

"Bad day?" She asked finally. Jason gave her a quick glance with his heavy eyes. "Ah. Got it," she said.

"It just seems to get worse every day. My job sucks. My ex is in love with someone else and, well, let's just say it's been nothing but downhill from there."

"It's a rough patch, but I like to think that as bad as life can get, it can get that much better. In fact, I believe in the theory that the more you suffer, the greater you will be rewarded. The pendulum effect."

"Well, if you're right, then I have one hell of a pay day coming. It would just be nice if it would get here soon."

"It never comes when you need it. Only when you're ready for it."

"Not very comforting."

"Sorry. I'm watching the Foster's kids. We were just about to fix some S'mores. Care to join?"

"Thanks, but no. I think I just want to be alone tonight."

"Suit yourself. You know where I am if you change your mind."

"I do." Jason said with a smile that sent Heather back out the door.

When it began to get darker, Jason realized that it was about time to eat. He got up and went for the kitchen when he realized he hadn't been shopping in days. He had no food left. He looked out the window and it looked like the rain was safely depleted. There was a small corner store a block away that was a bit over priced, but convenient. Jason grabbed his wallet and keys and dashed out the door. He passed his bike which was still laying, crumpled, on the lobby floor as he left the building. The cool air hit him like a knife. He ran down the steps and hurried down the street to the store.

He walked in and saw one clerk behind the counter. They exchanged weak glances and Jason moved toward the back of the store to the freezers. There were four doors that displayed a wide variety of beers and one that had a miniscule sampling of frozen entrees. Jason scanned quickly and just snagged the cheapest package he could find. He grabbed a six pack of beer for good measure and headed for the counter to pay for his items.

As he approached the cashier, two men walked in. They were dressed in dark shirts and were wearing hats. One was wearing a red hat and the other was wearing a white one. They moved quietly through the door. Before Jason could say another word, both men pulled out guns. The one in the red hat held his toward the cashier and the other one covered the door.

"Don't even breathe! Just empty the register and bag it all up!" He barked. Jason looked over and caught the thug's eye. "What are you looking at, asshole?" He barked. Jason looked away.

"Hurry up!" The gunman at the door yelled. The cashier's hands were shaking as he tried to get the drawer of the register to open. Red hat moved around the counter and pushed the barrel of his gun into the cashier's back.

"Please! Don't kill me! I have a wife! Children!" He begged.

"Don't worry, Abdul. You just hand over the green and this will all just be a bad memory." Red hat said. Jason stepped back slowly. He heard a click and looked over at the gun man at the door.

"Don't move," he said. Jason began to feel a strange sensation come over him. His arms began to tingle.

"I think I need to sit down," Jason said.

"You're not going anywhere. Cover this loser!" White hat said. Red looked over at Jason.

"Are you going to be a trouble maker? If you are, we can just blow those brains right out of you now." Red said as he turned his gun at Jason.

"Sorry. I'm just nervous."

"Get over it! We'll be done in just a minute," the cashier finished bagging the money and then Red took it. "Thanks. Good night." Red said as he cocked the gun and pointed it at the cashier's head.

"No!" The cashier cried. Suddenly, a shock ran through Jason's arm and he felt a cool sensation come over him. He looked over and black liquid began to seep out of his pores. His arm was quickly covered in an inky tar. A hard jolt burst through his arm and fired out of his hand in a shower of blue energy. The bolt flew wild across the room, but managed to find Red's gun. His arm flew up and he blasted into the ceiling. The cashier dove under the counter.

"What the hell?" Red said as he turned. The black liquid went back into Jason, but he could feel it swirling around in his blood. Red turned to Jason and stalked toward him. "What the hell are you doing?" He asked. Jason was having trouble keeping his footing.

"I told you I had to sit down," Another twinge struck him and his leg was enveloped by the dark liquid. Red jumped back in horror. Red turned and quickly headed for the door, but at last, the rest of the liquid burst out of Jason and his body was encased in the dark matter. It quickly formed into a second skin all over his body. Jason remembered the sensation from the other night. He looked over and saw both robbers running out the door, but his arms flew out instinctively and more blue energy poured out through his finger-tips. Red and White were both pulled back into the store. They flew back and Jason grabbed them both by their necks. The strength he was wielding was intoxicating. Both men felt no more heavy than a couple of shopping bags filled with marshmallows. They were screaming and crying.

Suddenly they remembered they still had their guns and fired at Jason's torso, but when the smoke cleared, their bullets hung in the air in little blue bubbles of light. Jason spun around and threw both thugs across the store and into the back wall. They hit hard and fell to the floor, unconscious. Jason walked over and looked down on them. They were out. He then turned and caught a glimpse of his reflection in the freezer. He was almost in shock. He had an idea of his appearance in the dark liquid, but only from images in his subconscious or in his many odd dreams. He had never seen his new form when he was totally aware.

The suit, as it appeared to be, seemed to form around him and enhanced certain attributes. His frame was larger and more muscu-lar. He touched his chest and it felt like there was nothing between his fingers and his body. Whatever he was covered in, was as thin as air, but seemingly as strong as steel. Suddenly, a cool sensation came over him and he could feel the suit break apart and retreat back into his body. Just as the last of the liquid seeped back into his skin, the cashier rose from behind the counter. His eyes were wide and he was still shaking.

"Where are they?" he asked. Jason indicated to the floor.

"They're kind of out. I think you should call the police. Fast."

"I will. Thank you,"

"Sure. Now." Jason said as he went back to the counter and attempted to resume his transaction.

"Uh, on the house."

"You sure?"

"Yes. Please. With my gratitude." Jason took his items and walked out the door.

As Jason approached his apartment building, he could hear the faint sound of police sirens growing stronger.

9

Jason's mind was a whirlwind of thought for most of the evening. He tried to distract himself with television, but it was no use. Something had clicked on in his mind when the suit emerged from his body. It had been the first time it had done anything while he was conscious. He looked down at his arm and even though he couldn't actually feel it or see it, he was more aware of its presence than ever. It was more than just something in his veins. It had become a part of him. As he thought longer, the meaning of his dreams began to become more clear. The dots were beginning to connect and it was as though a sense of total understanding had washed over Jason in the blink of an eye. The accumulated wisdom and knowledge of whatever was in him assumed into his own mind and was as much a part of him as his own memories and experiences.

What Jason found more troubling was how readily he accepted this truth. There was no fear in his heart and no trepidation in his soul. The picture was finally complete and he was okay with it. It was almost as if deep within, he was expecting it to happen.

Jason shut the TV off and walked on to his bedroom. He looked out the window and he could see a bright full moon hanging over the main skyline of Towers City. He could feel a new energy within him. Something that was echoing a quiet whisper in the back of his head. He looked over to his bed, but he wasn't anywhere near tired. He slipped on his shoes and hurried out.

Jason snuck up to the roof where he was able to get a better look at the moon. The commotion of the city was little more than a distant echo from the roof of his home. He could see the lights flashing from across the bay. Eagerness began to consume him. He could feel a throbbing in his wrists. He looked down and the veins he could see in the surface of his skin were slowly swelling. An unspeakable excitement began to bubble up to his head. He felt the liquid begin to urge slowly through his pores. A moment of panic took him, but suddenly, he relaxed and allowed it.

He felt the black liquid slide out of his skin and wrap around him tightly. It was strangely comforting to him. He felt a rush as it slid up the back of his neck and swallowed up his head. His vision was blocked, but suddenly two slits opened and the world was clear to him. Far more clear than it ever had been. Everything looked sharper and more alive to him. He took a step forward and he became more aware of his body. He looked down and the shiny dark fluid clung to his flesh like a new skin. He ran his fingers along his legs and they were hard. A lot harder than they normally were. It was like a layer of pure muscle had encased him, but he was so connected, it felt like his own body.

The fluid was thick over his body, but Jason could feel the faint, cool air of the night. His skin trembled as a shock of cold ran up his spine. He suddenly noticed a light come from above accompanied by the sound of loud propellers. A police helicopter came flying over. Jason quickly dashed into a nearby shadow, in hopes of hiding. He also heard the loud screech of tires on the street below. He ran over to the edge of the roof and saw a red car quickly slide around the corner and zoom down the street. Two police cars were close behind.

As if by instinct, Jason ran to follow the chase. He leapt high as he came to the end of the roof and landed easily on top of the neighboring building. He felt his legs pumping hard as he tried to keep up with the speeding car. He kept jumping from one building to the next, effortlessly. As he came to a building several stories higher than the others, he could feel a force shoot through him and his body floated up quickly to the top. As he landed, he had a second to realize what he had done, but his attention was captured again by the race on the streets below. He looked down and saw the red car far ahead of the police.

It was swerving recklessly as it careened through several busy intersections. Jason began running quickly and before he reached the end of the roof, he bent his legs and pushed forward hard. He shot up like a bullet and he felt a powerful force hold him in the air and launch him forward. Soon, he was high above the red car, keeping up with its pace easily. He shot ahead several blocks and landed on the tallest building he could see. He then held his arm out and with nothing more than a thought, a shock of blue light blasted out from his fingertips and hit the red car. After the tendrils of electricity died away, the red car came to a full stop. The driver seemed to try to bring the car back to life, but was unable to do so. Just as he began to get out of the red car, the police were on him. The copter above was hovering around and circling close. Jason crept back into the darkness and watched intently as the criminal was stuffed into one of the patrol cars and driven off to face his fate.

Jason was able to slip away from the crime scene under the cover of darkness and made his way back home. The suit slipped back into his body and he went back to his apartment. As he walked in, he switched on the TV and saw a breaking news bulletin about a high speed car chase that ran through the better part of the city and ended a few blocks away under what witnesses were calling 'mysterious circumstances'. Some claimed to have seen a bolt of lightning hit the pursued car while a few others said they saw a figure high above them. Most of those reports were argued away as nothing but attention getting rants from local screw jobs.

Suddenly Tyler came on the screen, as he was one of the officers involved with the chase. He asserted that there was nothing unusual about the apprehension of the suspect, but Jason knew Tyler enough to know there was a sense of doubt in his tone. He had seen something but he wasn't saying. Jason shut the TV off and went to his bed, tired at last. He climbed into his bed and soon his eyes closed and he had a calm, dreamless sleep.

The next morning, Jason awoke feeling more refreshed than he had in a long time. He quickly dressed and went out to the kitchen to fix his breakfast. As he fetched the milk out of the fridge he took a glance at his work schedule and according to it, he was off from the cafe and as Jason poured the cereal into his bowl, he had the idea to take the time to look into finding a more reliable job somewhere else.

He settled on the couch to eat his meal. He switched on the TV as he scooped some of his cereal into his mouth and saw that the attention getting rants from the night before had become wildfire rumors on the morning news.

More witnesses were coming out stating that they had also seen a shadowy figure on the rooftops the night before. Some said they saw the blast of energy that disabled the runaway car come from said figure while others were claiming they saw it flying through the air over their buildings. One woman even went as far as to draw a crude, but strangely accurate, rendering of Jason in his suit.

He switched the channel only to find the exploits of the mysterious figure was the hot topic on all the other news shows. He settled on a channel and watched intently. No one was saying much, but it was clear a fire had been lit, and everyone was talking about it.

He switched over to another channel and felt his stomach drop. They were in the middle of playing some grainy security camera footage. He quickly recognized the image of the little convenience store from the other night. He had seen the camera but it quickly slipped from this thoughts. He didn't even think it was really on.

"As you can see, the assailants come in from the front." The anchorwoman said over the footage. She was doing her best to explain what was going on. "They threaten the cashier and then they see someone out of frame. It's clear at this point they are all heavily armed."

The video quality wasn't very good. The punks all looked to be nothing more than amorphous blobs walking around. Suddenly, the picture completely fuzzed out and returned. With Jason front and center, outfitted with the suit. A few seconds more and the picture went black and they cut back to the anchorperson. "Wow. We apologize for the quality of the video but even still, I think we all saw enough to know what was happening."

"Now, Karen," The male anchor chimed in. "Do you really think there is an honest to God superhero in Towers City?"

"I know how crazy it may seem, Rich, but you saw with your own two eyes. Plus, let's not forget what happened during that high speed chase last night."

"I admit, it looked interesting, but how do we know it's not some publicity stunt? We really didn't see anything happen. That could have just been some nut job in tights pulling some elaborate prank to get a little TV exposure."

"As of now, there is no official comment from anyone. Even the store owner was unable to give any more insight, but we will be following this story as it develops." Karen said.

"If it develops." Rich added quickly as he shuffled his papers on the desk. "Sports is next with an interview with the Towers Trouncers' star quarterback, Seth Markinson. Find out about his future plans after his current, record-breaking season." Jason quickly shut the TV off and set his breakfast down.

"They didn't see anything. Nothing. That guy doesn't know me. He doesn't know where I live." Jason reassured himself. He got up and looked out the window. There didn't seem to be any commotion. "There's no way they could have known it was me."

After Jason finished his meal, he dressed and put together a loose plan for finding a better job. As he stepped out of his door, he heard Heather's door open and soon he heard her voice call out to him.

"Morning, neighbor," Jason turned and Heather was able to take him in. "Wow. You look nice," she said as she pointed to his ensemble. Jason was dressed in a nice buttoned up dress shirt and a pair of gray slacks. His hair was combed neatly and arranged carefully across his scalp.

"Thanks. I gotta pound the pavement and get a new job."

"Things not working out at the cafe?"

"It's great there. It's just there isn't enough work. I thought if I could get another job somewhere else, that would help balance things out. Just enough so I can make rent without breaking a sweat, you know?"

"Good thinking. Did you see the news this morning?"

"Uh, No. Anything interesting?"

"They're saying there's a superhero in town."

"What?"

"They had some security footage from a little store a few blocks away. I don't know if it was for real. It doesn't seem like it could be possible."

"Seems pretty out there."

"I know, but it wouldn't be the first time in this town. I mean, you're new here, but Towers City seems like a lightning rod for strange occurrences."

"I always thought the crime rate here was pretty low."

"I didn't say anything about crime. There's just something about this town. I've heard about a drug going around the club circuit that gives people super powers."

"Is that possible?"

"Anything is possible. Trust me. A superhero blowing into town isn't totally out of the question."

"Even if it were true, why here? Why not New York or Chicago?"

"I don't know. Why did the Big Bang hurl this chunk of rock we call Earth the exact distance from the sun so that it could sustain life? Why anything? I don't waste too much time asking pointless questions. I believe in dealing with what truly is."

"Sounds good. I better get going."

"Sure. Good luck."

"Thanks!" Jason said as he dashed down the stairs.

Jason spent the better part of the day downtown going in and out of all the stores asking for applications. He wasn't thrilled with the idea of returning to retail, but he had reached his crisis point. He dropped applications at overly pretentious clothing salons and body care shops. Many of the shops he visited had very strong artistic vibes with loud industrial music playing and model perfect clients.

He finally came to one of the larger department stores in town, Vermont's. It was not only large, but it was one of the oldest department stores in the country. The facade outside had been constructed in an art deco style to reflect its age and style. Jason walked in and it was eerily quiet. There weren't too many shoppers and the staff on the sales floor seemed to be rather listless. The perfume department sprawled out before him as he walked through the glass doors. The faint scent of flowers and spices lilted through the air. He approached a sales woman who seemed to be rather bored.

"Excuse me?" He asked. The sales woman turned her head towards Jason but her expression stayed fixed.

"Yes?"

"I'd like a job application, please," The sales woman's lips pulled at the corners as if she was trying to smile.

"Check with the administration desk,"

"Where...?"

"Back there." The woman said. Jason looked over her shoulder and he could only see an ocean of designer labels. He merely nodded to the sales woman and continued on his way.

He walked through the maze of counters and make over stations and soon he could see a small alcove far in the back, behind the men's clothing section. He approached it and saw it was the office and customer service area. There was an old sign built into the wall which listed what departments were inside and administration was clearly printed on the bottom.

Jason walked in and it was like a tomb inside. The room looked like it was the one part of the store that hadn't been touched in all the years of renovation. The walls were a soft pink and it seemed like the carpet was as old as the building, as it had dark smears and marks all over it. There were no customers and the two women behind the counter were so fully immersed in their conversation, neither noticed Jason's entrance. The other windows were closed. Jason turned a corner and he saw a door with the word 'administration' on it. He walked over and put his hand on the knob and pushed, but it didn't budge. He tried pulling, but again, nothing.

"It's closed, sir." Jason heard a voice calling from behind. He turned and saw one of the women who failed to notice him earlier was poking her head out and calling after him.

"What?"

"You want administration?"

"Yes."

"They're closed. What did you want?"

"A job application." Jason said as he began to approach the woman. As she came into full view, she bent down and quickly pulled out a piece of paper and slid it over to Jason.

"Here," she said flatly. Jason looked up intending to thank her, but as he looked up, the woman had already resumed her conversation with her co-worker. Jason took the application and headed out but stopped suddenly. He didn't feel like going home, so he pulled out the pen he was holding in his pocket and sat down in a nearby chair to fill the application out.

He quickly filled in his basic information and just as he was getting to the education section, there was a strange commotion outside. He quickly got up and peered around the corner. Suddenly, a gun shot rang out and was followed by a chorus of panicked screams. The few customers in the store had been gathered together in the middle of the sales floor and they were all cowering like sheep. Then Jason heard the sound of boots walking along a tile floor. He glanced over and saw two women with guns approaching. They were both dressed in a style that would suit a rock star more than a petty thief.

They both had big, wild black hair with shocks of green and red running along the sides. Their skirts were short and torn and adorned with oversized buckles and rhinestones. They both held large rifles in their arms and as soon as he saw that, he jumped back and found cover. He got out of sight just as a shot blasted in. The women behind the windows stopped talking and started screaming. Soon, the screaming stopped and he could hear voices outside.

"Just stay down and shut up and no one loses her head!" A forceful voice barked and then the sound of a gun being cocked was heard. Jason stood up as he realized they couldn't see him and soon a familiar feeling began to come over him. His skin was getting warmer and before he knew it, the black liquid was seeping through his pores, but there was no panic in Jason's heart. He welcomed the liquid.

The sensation of it coursing through his veins and bleeding through his skin was exhilarating. The cool sensation of the fluid slipping over his skin and tightening gently over his body was not unpleasant. As the dark gel enveloped his head, his eyes were blocked, but quickly two shafts of light appeared and soon his vision returned. In fact, it was better than normal. As he looked around the room, everything looked sharper and more detailed. He quickly examined his body, still marveling at the sensation of the dark suit.

"Doors are locked and no one upstairs. Let's hurry." Another voice said. Jason's hearing was remarkably improved as well. It sounded like the voices were just inches away. He turned toward the wall and as he concentrated on the wall, his vision darkened and he was able to make out strange colored lights through the wall. A large group of red lights on the left and two orange whisps moving around on the right. Jason shook his head slightly and realized he was seeing heat signatures. He blinked quickly and his vision returned to normal. He tried to think of a plan of action. Jumping in and startling the two gun women could lead to a very ugly situation, he thought. He had to sneak up on them, but it wasn't going to be easy. Jason inched toward the threshold between the alcove and the store. He peered around and got a better look at the two robbers. They looked familiar and just like that it hit him as to where he saw them. They were Delia and Darla Gunner. Two sisters who formed a hard rock duo known as Twinister.

They had a reputation for raucous behavior and wild clothes. They had a few run ins with the press and it seemed they were always punching or kicking someone or getting into some kind of trouble on a routine basis. He remembered they had a big hit once and it looked like they were going to be the next big thing, but their first album tanked and they fell into obscurity as quickly as they had risen.

A few years after that, they emerged again but instead of singing, they were holding up liquor stores, but were still acting like the rock stars they might have been. Over the years, their criminal career grew more than their music had. Their first big bust came when they went on a four state crime spree robbing banks and just about anyone they could find for over a month. Police from over six counties tracked them down and they held up in a cheap motel just outside of Phoenix. The standoff lasted for a week and they did not go quietly.

Jason felt a rush of urgency. Neither Darla nor Delia had anything to lose. In fact, the worse things got, the more they would like it, so he knew he had to take them out and fast. He crept forward along the floor. He stopped for a second and realized he had gone unseen. He continued toward a small staircase not too far away. When he got upstairs he saw there was a terrace that afforded a perfect view of the sales floor below. He looked down and saw all the customers crouched together. Delia had her gun trained on them while Darla was busy in the jewelry department going through the cases. She bashed down on each case with her gloved hand and gathered up as much jewelry as she could hold.

"This stuff is cheap as hell!" Darla said as she grabbed a tiara. She quickly inspected it and then pressed it between her hands until the band snapped, sending little diamonds to fly all over the place. "Hardly worth robbing this dump."

"I know." Delia said as she turned to three mannequins set up behind her, dressed in some lovely Spring fashions. She aimed her rifle quickly and blasted the one on the end. "Ugly," she said and looked to the middle one and blasted it. Just as she was about to blast the last one, Darla ran over and stopped her.

"No. I have that skirt," Delia nodded and quickly shot the torso of the mannequin off.

"Why are you doing this!?" One of the hostages said as she stood up. Jason noticed it was the snooty sales woman who he encountered when he came in. "If anyone walks in, they'll call the police and there's no way you'll get out of here if that happens!" she said. Darla walked up to her and jammed the barrel of her rifle against the sales woman's neck.

"Listen, grandma! We take what we want! If cops come, it'll be their funerals. And yours. Now sit down before I break your damn legs!" She barked. The sales woman quickly returned to the floor as Darla rejoined her sister.

"Keep things under control out here. I'm going for the safe." They both stepped further away from the hostages and Jason saw his chance, but just as he was about to move, a loud voice shot out from outside.

"Darla and Delia Gunner! This is the police! Come out with your hands up!" An stern voice barked. Darla and Delia sprang towards the front door and looked outside. Police cars lined the street and had blocked off the road. They stood back.

"Cops." Darla said.

"How'd they know?" They turned to the hostages and started

pushing through and inspecting each one. They finally came to a pretty blonde woman. It was Bethany Lauvre. Her hair was shining and glistening perfection, but her eyes were puffy and red from crying. She was holding a cell phone in her hand. They quickly took it from her and discovered she had dialed for the police.

"Pretty slick, bitch."

"Hey. She looks familiar." Delia said. Darla regarded Bethany carefully.

"Yeah. You famous?" Bethany suddenly lit up and tossed her hair to her left, which she had often claimed was her signature move.

"Yes, as a matter of fact. I host Good Morning Towers."

"Right. The squeaky, annoying bitch with the annoying show. God, I hate your voice. It's like nails in my brain."

"I guess you don't want an autograph." Darla quickly pressed her gun to Bethany's head.

"No, but I wouldn't mind blowing your brains all over the walls right now!" Darla said. Bethany howled in fear and crumpled to the floor.

"Throw out your guns and surrender to the police! If you do not comply within the next five minutes..." The booming voice called out. Darla spun around and blasted two shots outside.

"Take your best shot, pigs!" She spat. Darla looked over at Delia who was still threatening Bethany. She marched over and grabbed Delia away. "Forget her. We need to get that money and out of here now," she said.

"They've got us surrounded. How are we going to get through all that?" Delia asked.

"I don't know, but we'll do it. We're Twinister! We're bad!"

"We're bad." They then both high fived each other. It sounded like they had both distanced themselves from the hostages, so Jason made his move. He flipped over the terrace and landed squarely between the hostages and Twinister. Darla and Delia both stepped back, clearly surprised by his appearance. Panic gripped Jason. He wasn't sure what to do next, but he felt a surge of endorphins running through him. It was like he was on the crest of the wave and he knew he couldn't stop.

"Bad? I'll say. You two should be locked up for those outfits alone," They both eased their expressions and lifted up their guns.

"Well, sister dear," Darla began. "Look who's playing fashion police."

"He's one to talk." Delia added. They both quickly fired their weapons, but Jason spun away and they were only able to take out a cash register. Jason leapt forward, away from the hostages, and Delia and Darla continued firing at him. Glass and make up flew up into the air and landed on the floor as Jason scrambled for cover. When they stopped he bolted up and a surge of blue energy shot through his arms and poured out in a hard beam. He connected with the guns and was able to pull them out of Darla and Delia's hands with just a flick of his wrist. Jason was ready to chase after them, but instead of running from him, they charged at him. Darla leapt up and landed a hard kick right in his chest while Delia jumped up on his back and started pounding his head with her fists. Jason spun around clumsily and slapped Darla way. He then grabbed Delia's legs and threw her off his back with ease. They were running up at him again when he fired a wild beam which grabbed a large metal display case and he was able to hurl it at them, smashing them to the floor. Jason quickly lifted the case away and saw that both women were still intact, but out cold. The sound of several footsteps approaching could be heard. Jason looked over his shoulder and saw the police rushing forward, so he quickly dashed out of sight.

Jason raced through the store and found the stock room in the back. He could hear the talking and activity growing behind him and he wasn't ready to be seen as he was. He felt the suit go back into his body just as he found a small door in the back of the stock room that led outside into a small alley on the side of the street. He ran out and caught his breath. He hurried to the street and much to his relief, he saw that there was so much going on, no one noticed one non-descript man walking by. He saw Twinister being loaded up into a nearby ambulance and a sense of satisfaction filled him. He quickly put as much distance between him and the store as he could.

That night, Jason relaxed for a quiet night in. He felt he had been through enough excitement for one day. He decided he'd stay in and watch a nice relaxing movie. He chose a guilty pleasure film that always managed to make him feel good and just as he was settling on his couch with a bag of popcorn, he saw a short news break on TV. It was amateur video of Twinister's robbery attempt. Jason felt the bottom of his world fall when he saw himself appear on screen, dressed in the black suit.

"And this crude video, captured by KTWR's own Bethany Lauvre, was taken just this afternoon when the lethal criminals known as Twinister attempted to rob Vermont's in a daring daytime robbery. Little did they know Towers City now has its very own super hero, as is clearly seen here." The anchor woman said as the video played and showed every moment of the standoff as it happened, with Jason in clear view.

10

The video Bethany leaked to the press had spread like wild fire all over town. The grainy video was shown on the local news venues on a near regular basis. The newspapers began following the story and the Towers Tribune was offering a hefty reward for any pictures of the costumed hero. Each day, an article lauding him as a hero or warning against his evil could be found in the opinions section. The press had begun calling him Spectrum, as some leading scientists asserted that his powers were electromagnetically based. Jason was instantly uncomfortable with the media frenzy surrounding his new alter ego but at the same time he felt a bit of a boost that he had been able to cause such a stir, but then, he thought, anyone with the suit would have caused the same stir.

Not all the attention Spectrum was receiving was from journalists and celebrity personalities. In a large dilapidated building in a section of Towers' downtown area known as the Phantom Projects, a weathered figure sat in what could only be defined as a lair, deep in thought.

Sur Reel sat in a small chair surrounded by a stuffed bear and a beaten up plush rabbit with a torn ear. He was slumped and brooding. He was a tall, thin creature dressed in a worn out, black and red pin striped suit with a black top hat that cast a shadow over his milky gray eyes. He was lost in thought as he recalled the past fifty years he had spent on Earth.

He had landed on Earth in the womb of a baby comet that crashed along a lonely highway in the northwest. As he emerged from the ice and fire of his transport, he quickly discovered his divine form could not be sustained and he feared he would die, but as he felt his weakened life force fading away, he had a visitor. A mortal by the name of Leonard Fellus. Sur Reel would later discover that Leonard was a third rate illusionist who happened to be driving home from another failed magic show at a nearby restaurant. He fancied offering the patrons of certain dining establishments some entertainment to go along with their meal. That night in particular, he ruined a young man's plan to propose to his girlfriend and upset another woman by reminding her of the death of a beloved pet. He concluded the show by inadvertently smashing a small rabbit with a large mallet in front of a small audience of children. He had been tossed out of the building and warned never to return. As he drove along, trying to figure out where he went wrong, he was startled by a loud explosion off the side of the road. He stopped and found a large hole where the comet had landed. He approached the crater and found Sur Reel's weakening body. As Sur Reel awoke, he saw what he needed to do. He took hold of Leonard and transferred his life force into his body, like a crab taking over a new shell. His mind and energy took over and replaced Leonard's. He soon felt the unique sensation of being flesh and blood. He did not care for it at first, but as the years went on, he learned as best he could and studied the habits of mortals.

Sur Reel found it endlessly curious the obsession of mortals for colored paper they referred to as money. As a God, he traded in power, but on Earth, money seemed to replace power as the leading currency. He saw men die for the chance to own large amounts of it, but saw very little good come from any of it. Sur Reel's body held up very well for a long time, but after thirty years, he noticed it was beginning to show signs of fatigue.

Sur Reel's powers were able to keep the body alive, but not all together. His flesh was rotting and his joints and hinges were weak and broken. He was staring at a finger on his left hand he had to tape back on three times that year.

He had grown weary of his post, searching for the anomaly he was charged with finding, but with the arrival of Spectrum, he began to think his time among the mortals was numbered. He looked over at the bear sitting to his right.

"Well, Mr. Marbles. I called, but there's really no way to know if she'll ever come." Suddenly, the door swung open and a beautiful woman with dark hair and wearing a sharp suit came in. Sur Reel stood, his dark, gray eyes squinting and his lips curled into a terrible smile. "You're late."

"You do not dictate terms to us." Hither said as she walked in, inspecting the room. Her expression made it clear she did not approve.

"It would be nice to know that someone out there was paying attention!" Sur Reel barked as he stood to his full height. His aged skin pulled against his bones. "Hither. You look good as a mortal. Where do you put the wings?"

"Let's just get this over with. You said you found the anomaly?"

"Yes!" Sur Reel said and pointed to the small, run down television set that sat in the corner. The screen came on and the video of Spectrum's heroic deed played over. When it was done, Sur Reel looked back to Hither, expectant. Her face was unmoved. "They call him Spectrum."

"That's it?"

"What do you mean 'that's it?'? There's your anomaly!"

"How do you figure that?"

"A human ape with powers like that? You don't think that's a little bit of a red light? I mean, if that's not an anomaly, I don't know what is!"

"The presence of a human being with extra normal abilities does not indicate any kind of irregularity. The Design works in mysterious ways."

"Well, then go ask The Design if a human in black tights firing energy from his hands was in the plan." Sur Reel argued. Hither turned away from him quickly and walked over to the one window that wasn't completely covered in dirt and dust.

"I admit, it could be something."

"Yes! It could be! When do I get sprung?"

"I never said anything about your debt being repaid."

"Come on! I've been stuck on this dust ball too long as it is! Look at this body! This is what I've been reduced to!" Sur Reel said as he tore his finger off his hand. "These bodies are pathetic! Two or three decades and they start falling apart!"

"Be that as it may, we need to be certain this is the anomaly."

"What do you need?"

"We need to know the extent of his powers. You have to find out what this Spectrum is all about. How strong is he? How do his powers work?"

"And then I'm free?"

"Possibly. Bring the proof that is needed to confirm this, and I will discuss with Sanctum the possibility of releasing you."

"All right, but to get this done, I'm going to need a little bit more of my power back."

"Absolutely not."

"How am I supposed to deal with this guy like this? With a little more juice I can put him through his paces." Hither regarded him carefully.

"Fine, but only a bit more."

"Fine. Just give it to me." Hither approached Sur Reel and placed her hand to his forehead. A small glow emitted from her palm and flowed into Sur Reel's head. She pulled away quickly.

"There. When you have discovered what we need, contact me. Not before." Hither said and spun around on her heel and hurried out through the door.

PART 2

11

The wind was strong and the rain was coming down hard. Like little, icy knives cutting through the air. I found my perch at the top of one of the taller buildings downtown. I looked below and I could barely see the street. I began to wonder how the heroes in comic books ever found any crime being up so high.

I had taken to going on patrol late at night. Every time I caught myself thinking of Tyler and David together, I felt the need to do something to distract myself and flying around the city was as good idea as any, I thought. It was also a good way to get used to using the suit and every night, I seemed to learn something new. I knew I could fly, I could fire electric bolts and I could generate and control intense magnetic fields. I wasn't even totally sure how I was doing it. I just thought of what I wanted to do and I did it. I had checked some science books out at the library, but it was all way over my head.

I stepped off the edge of the building and flew down so I could get a better look at the streets below. Using the suit had quickly become second nature to me. I shifted into my flying mode with barely a thought. It felt like I had an electric bubble in the middle of my stomach and it kept me afloat. I got as close as I could without being seen.

Buzz surrounding Spectrum had died down a bit, but it was still the biggest story in town. The news still kept chatting about new sightings and every day the paper would run at least three pages of letters from people who either supported me or feared that I was the beginning of a global catastrophe. As the days crawled along, public opinion would shift slightly and it seemed it was leaning in my favor, but while the public had seemed to grow accustomed to their new hero, the police weren't quite so accommodating.

Police Chief Kelvin was quick to issue an arrest warrant despite my obviously benign actions. At first, that kept me in but after stopping a couple more muggings and hate crimes, I began to see the city really needed someone out there. The city needed me, and I began to realize I needed it as well.

The few times I took up the suit, I felt something I hadn't ever felt before. I felt important. I felt like I was making a difference, and I had never known I needed to feel that way, but I did. Serving coffee in a chic coffee house was fine, but in the long run, it was nothing. No one ever needed a cup of coffee. No one's life hung in the balance over a low fat blueberry muffin. It was like a whole layer of who I was became clear to me. I wanted to help. I wanted to make a difference. I wanted to be a hero.

On the whole, Towers City enjoyed a very low crime rate, but there were always a few brushfires popping up here and there that just fell through the cracks. I felt this was where I was needed most.

The rain was growing heavier and the streets were practically abandoned. I looked down at my wrist and the suit parted away enough so that I could see my watch. It was almost three in the morning and I hadn't found any trouble. I decided to call it a night, or morning. I flew up high over the skyline in order to avoid being spotted by the police and soared over the clouds back to my place.

I landed on the roof, changed back and snuck inside. It was all very routine to me. I crept to my door, but just as I was walking in, I heard the door behind me open.

"Hey!" Heather called out. I spun around and there she was in

a cow print bathrobe. "I haven't seen you in ages. How are you?"
I froze. I hadn't expected to see anyone, which was why I wasn't
wearing anything but a t shirt and some boxers.

"I've been okay." I said. Heather's eyes ran up and down quickly
and she smiled slightly.

"So, that's what you've been up to,"

"What?" I panicked.

"You've been hitting the gym. You look fantastic," she said as she
reached over and squeezed my bicep. I looked down and was a little
surprised myself.

"Uh, yeah. I guess I haven't really noticed." I said. My body had
changed a lot, but that was the first time I had noticed. My arms
were bigger and my chest was thicker. How did I not notice that?

"How could you not notice? When you moved in, you were
frumpy and slumped over. Now look at you! Muscles and everything. You still gay?"

"'Fraid so."

"Too bad. So what are you doing up so early and running around
in your underwear?"

"Just checking for the paper. Hasn't come yet."

"They leave the papers outside."

"Oh. That explains it. What are you doing up?" I asked quickly.

"I just heard some noises on the roof."

"I didn't. That's weird."

"I've been hearing noises up there for months now, but I guess
my curiosity is getting the best of me. It sounds like someone is
running around up there or something."

"Maybe something is loose. Like a duct or something."

"That's what I thought, but I've been checking all that stuff. I'm
just going to take a look again. Don't want to give whatever it is a
chance to escape."

"I wouldn't do that. It's cold and rainy outside." Heather looked
over at me with a glare of suspicion.

"How would you know? You look dry as a bone."

"I saw it raining outside. Through my window. I'm guessing about the cold. It probably is. Kinda chilly in here already." I said and flashed her an uneasy smile. She pulled her robe tight around her body.

"I guess you're right. Well, I better get back to sleep then."

"Right. I'll see you later."

"Later," she said as she went back into her apartment. I ran into mine and slammed the door shut behind me. I walked over to the bathroom and pulled my shirt off. I nearly fell over. My body had completely changed. I had thick, well proportioned muscles all over my torso and my waist was at least three inches leaner and for the first time in my life, I had abs! It had been so long and I was just then noticing the change.

"Did you do this?" I asked to the suit, half expecting an answer. I flexed a bit but then I felt fatigue coming on. I decided to hold off on my vanity and headed for bed.

As I laid my head down on the pillow, my eyes fell shut and I was deep in sleep almost instantly.

The next day at the Lauvre Cafe, I was busy going about my chores when I saw Tyler walk in without Dave, which made my heart skip a little bit faster.

"Morning." I said. Tyler almost did a double take as I approached him.

"Jason?" I then recalled we hadn't seen each other in months. The last time he had seen me, I wasn't the man I was then.

"Yeah. Nice, huh?"

"I'll say. You've been working out?"

"You could say that. Where's Dave?"

"In a meeting. Kelvin is appointing him to some special task force."

"What kind of task force?"

"I don't know. It's on a need to know basis. He said he'd meet me here when he was done." My heart fell a bit at that.

"Okay. Have a seat and I'll get you a cup of today's special. It's

Ethiopian, I think."

"Make it two?"

"Sure." I said. I hurried to the kitchen to fetch the coffee. As I poured, I could hear the front door open and the unmistakable sound of Dave's voice ring through the air. I finished up and quickly ran out with the cups. I saw Tyler and Dave sitting at a small table near the front of the cafe.

"Two of today's specials, coming up." I said as I set the cups down in front of Tyler and Dave.

"Hi, Jay. Nice to see you. Lookin' good. You hittin' the bench?" Dave asked.

"Must be all the sweeping I do here. Don't let me interrupt." I said and returned to my duties. I resumed wiping down the tables, but I was able to keep one ear open on their conversation.

"So, what did Kelvin want?"

"He wants me to head up a unit to deal with Spectrum."

"What?"

"You heard me. He wants me all over this thing. He's letting me pick my own team. I've got access to the choppers and everything. He told me to spare no expense in taking this freak down."

"Oh."

"Don't gush. What's the matter? This is a good thing. If I can take this Spectrum thing down, it's going to mean a big promotion!"

"I just don't think Spectrum is all that much of a threat. He's been doing a lot of good, actually."

"Towers City doesn't need some nut job in tights running around and making something out of nothing. Besides, you know how it is with these guys. They are like lightning rods for bigger freaks. If we don't stomp him down now, who knows what could come around here. Hell, he could be an alien! This could just be the beginning of some full scale invasion."

"You cannot seriously believe that."

"Well, if he's not a human, where's he get those powers from?"

"I don't know, but I don't think anyone who really meant us harm, alien or otherwise, would use his powers to stop muggers and hate crimes. I don't know where he came from or what he is, but I believe he's here to help. We should work with him."

"That's what he wants us to believe, but Kelvin's not playing into his hands that easily. We're taking him out, and that's that."

"And you're going to lead the charge."

"That's right."

"Why doesn't Kelvin take the lead on this himself?"

"He's got plenty more to worry about. Besides, he says he checked all the personnel files, and he found I am exactly the kind of soldier he needs for this fight."

"He said that? Soldier?"

"So what? Look, I came from the army. I know how this stuff works. You can't have some outsider making up his own rules. We have laws and the only way they work is if we all follow them."

"And if someone doesn't, we find them and kill them."

"Don't be so dramatic. We'll attempt to bring him in, but if he fights, I have been cleared to use lethal force. It's really up to him."

"I'll just bet."

"So, I take it we won't be celebrating this tonight."

"I'm happy for you, Dave. I'm happy that Kelvin trusts and believes in you enough to put you in charge of a big operation like this. I just don't happen to agree with said operation."

"That's too bad. I really needed a primary coordinator for this and I was thinking you'd be perfect."

"Primary coordinator?"

"You know. Right hand man. Strategist. You're the best at that kind of crap. I remember when you were called in when that psycho took those patients hostage at First Memorial. It was like a work of art."

"I was pretty damn good, wasn't I?"

"You were. You know me. I'm a 'shoot first, ask questions later' kinda guy. You balance me out. I need you with me on this." Dave said and then put his hand gently over Tyler's. I looked over quickly to Tyler. It looked like he was thinking hard on Dave's offer. I tried not to be obvious about it, but I was slowly shaking my head, hoping Tyler would pick up on it.

"If only to keep you from losing control. Fine. I'll do it." Tyler said with a pained expression on his face. Dave smiled and pulled Tyler into a kiss across the table. I felt my breakfast beg for release.

"Thank you!" Dave said.

They both continued drinking their coffee, but I was no longer interested in what they had left to say, so I paid them no mind. I barely noticed as they got up and left, leaving a healthy tip behind.

After my shift ended, I had only thoughts of going out again to try to put Tyler out of my head. I hurried home and got in a nap before dark. I ate a light dinner and Spectrum was on his way.

I flew over the city until I landed a few blocks from the club Skye. It didn't seem familiar at first, but after a while, I remembered. I slinked a few blocks over and I could see the club below. A large crowd was gathered in front and I could hear the music from inside. My night with Tyler and David flooded back into my mind. I think they were even playing a song that they played that night, but then most of the music they played at clubs all sounded the same to me.

I found a spot on the roof of a store front across the street which was well covered by shadow. I knew I had to leave. Everything in my soul knew it wasn't healthy to linger on the pain of my memory, but I couldn't resist. I suddenly heard a weak snap, like a camera taking a picture. I looked around quickly and saw a figure on the roof two units over. It was too dark to make out who it was, so I snuck over quietly through the abundant darkness. I was silent as a ninja. I was able to get just a few feet away when I quickly shot my arm out and grabbed onto the figure's shoulder and spun them around. It was a girl. She was wearing a long, dark coat and her hair was black and cropped short. She was sporting a pair of glasses and held a camera in her trembling hands. Her eyes were wide with surprise as I stood before her.

"Who are you?" I asked. She stepped back. The surprise in her face faded quickly away and she tensed her back and seemed to be staring me down.

"Ashley Chambers. Who are you?" She asked. I was a little surprised at her question, since it seemed for several weeks you couldn't go a day without hearing about Spectrum.

"Never mind." I wasn't totally comfortable using my hero name in any kind of conversation. "What are you doing here? Aren't Paparazzi supposed to be closer to the action?"

"I'm not one of the photo thugs. I'm a reporter for the Towers Weekly."

"Never heard of it."

"Underground paper. We delve deeper than the Tribune and find out the real, unfiltered truth about life here in Towers."

"So what brings you here tonight?"

"I don't see how that's any of your business. I have freedom of the press."

"Not unless you're stalking someone." I said and I stepped forward, but before I could even breathe, she whipped out a stun gun and pressed it against my arm and gave me a good charge. The suit seemed to react to it oddly. It shot back the electricity and caused a short but colorful light show in the alley. Ashley's stun gun fell to the ground and broke on impact. I could see once again I had caught her off guard. I decided quickly to take advantage of it. "What are you doing here?" I asked again, with a bit more authority.

"I'm just following up on a piece I'm doing about Neon."

"Neon? As in the lights?"

"No. Neon as in the deadly drug."

"Never heard of it." Ashley quickly reached into her pocket and pulled out a small glass vial filled with a bright, glowing liquid.

"This is Neon. It's the latest club drug. Right now, Towers is practically drowning in this stuff and no one's doing anything about it."

"It's toxic?"

"No. In fact, by all the tests that have been done, it's not even a drug of any kind. There are no addictive components at all."

"Non-addictive. Non-toxic. Sounds pretty safe to me. What's the harm?"

"We don't buy it."

"We?"

"The Towers Weekly. The deal is you drink a shot of this and you're in heaven for hours. You come down? Take another shot and you're flying again. The only problem is there are side effects they don't tell you about."

"Such as?"

"I covered a story a week ago about some guy who went into a coma after overdosing on Neon. When he woke up, he was able to shoot electricity out of his hands. I was only able to talk to him for a few minutes. When I came back to the hospital, he had checked out and no one there seemed to remember him ever being there."

"You think this is a cover up?"

"I don't know, but Neon is making things happen which may pose a threat to the general public and no one is talking about it. I've learned that Skye over there is one of the bigger hot spots for Neon dealers."

"Standing out here taking pictures isn't going to do much good."

"I'm waiting for my writing partner, Sam. He's in there trying to buy directly from Spyder."

"Spyder?"

"He's the main connection in town. He's the only person who gets his Neon directly from the supplier. We'll be able to track them down by going through him. At least I hope we can. We find them, expose Neon for the deadly menace it is and shut them down for good." Ashley said as she turned away and set her attention upon Skye once more. I stood there, feeling a bit perplexed.

"So, you're not even going to ask about the suit." I said. She waved her hand at me quickly.

"Yeah, Spectrum. I know. I don't live under a rock. Now be quiet." I was about to return to my perch high above, but she seemed to grow upset.

"What is it?"

"Spyder's leaving," I ran up behind her and she pointed out a slick looking guy with dark hair and lanky arms and legs. His clothes were rumpled and filthy, which helped him to stand out from the other trendy clubbers surrounding him.

"So?"

"Sam should have been out first. He was supposed to make contact, buy and then get out." Ashley quickly pulled out her phone and quickly dialed. "No answer. Something is wrong."

"You want me to go in and check it out?"

"You? Seriously? The goal here is to not call attention to ourselves. Thanks for the meet and greet. I wouldn't mind an interview sometime, but right now, I'm going down there to check on Sam. Good night," she said and quickly brushed by me. She headed over to a small, metal ladder that was built into the building and climbed down quickly. I watched as she dashed across the street and disappear into the crowd outside the club.

While I would be the first to admit I wasn't very experienced in the realm of crime solving or detection, I was beginning to get a feeling in the pit of my stomach that begged me to stay. I hunkered down and waited for something to happen, but after only fifteen minutes, my previous feeling was beginning to turn into a full out alarm. I gave the immediate area a quick glance and it was obvious I wouldn't be able to get anywhere near Skye without causing a riot. Instead, I decided to get a bird's eye view. I lifted up into the sky and drifted across to the club.

As I was about to land on the roof, I heard some noises coming from the parking lot in back. I went over and saw three figures in the shadows. One large figure was holding another, while the third stood before them both, yelling and screaming. I couldn't hear clearly what was being said, but then there was a blast of light and a blood curdling scream. I leapt down to the ground and as I did, one of the three dark figures turned to me. He was a young guy, trim build. His hair was bleached blonde and spiked up high. His expression was twisted in anger. His friend, a large, hulking thing, dropped whoever it was he was holding and stepped forward. He looked even more odd. His skin was a slight shade of green and his eyes were yellow. I barely noticed he had a long, thin forked tongue slipping in and out between his clenched teeth, as he smiled a sick grin.

"What's the trouble here?"

"None of your business. Now get the hell out of here!" The spiked haired boy said. I looked down and whoever his large friend was holding against his will, looked to be dead to me.

"What's with your friend? A little too much partying?"

"No. He partied just enough." Suddenly the door to the club behind us opened and I heard Ashley's voice.

"Jared?" She asked in sincere shock. The kid with spiked hair reacted quickly.

"Ash, what the hell are you doing here?" He asked. Ashley ran past me to Jared.

"What am I doing here? What about you? Where have you been? You've been off the radar for over a month! What is going on here?"

"It's none of your business! Now, if you know what's good for you, you'll forget you saw me here and never come back!"

"How can you say that? Jared! I've missed you so much." Ashley said as she nearly broke tears. She stepped forward to throw her arms around Jared, but he was quick to push her back.

"It's different now."

"What is?"

"Everything! I told them to tell you I was dead. You weren't supposed to find me."

"Why not?"

"I've got a new life, Ash. A new life you can't be a part of. I know you can't see it now, but I'm doing you a favor here. Just walk away, or else this is going to get messy."

"Jared." I could hear the tears in her trembling voice. "I don't understand." She looked down quickly and I noticed her posture shifted. She had noticed the body on the ground. "Is that Sam?" She asked as she stooped down.

"He was asking questions." Jared said.

"He was here to find out about Neon."

"Yeah," Ashley stood back up and turned to Jared slowly.

"You're working for them now, aren't you? The monsters who are pushing this stuff. You're their muscle now."

"You don't understand, Ash. You have no idea the power I feel. It's like I've just now started living. I was just hoping it didn't have to go down like this."

"What are you talking about?" Ashley asked. Jared lifted his hand up and suddenly sparks began to shoot up from his fingers. Raw bolts of electricity filled the air. Ashley slowly stepped back and bumped into the green guy, who jerked his head at her and bared two rather large fangs on either side of his mouth. She shrieked and jumped away. I ran to her and pushed her behind, putting me between her and Jared and his friend.

"Just walk away, man. This isn't your fight." Jared said.

"There's no fight here at all. You're just going to let the lady go on her way."

"Too late for that. She knows too much. That's always been her problem, you know? A real snoop. She just doesn't know how to leave well enough alone."

"You killed that man."

"He had an accident. Very tragic. Now, step aside."

"I'm not going anywhere."

"Then I guess there is a fight here after all." Jared said and suddenly his arm shot out and latched onto my shoulder. I felt a sudden jolt of energy rip through me. My vision was blurred with light. My blood began to race and I felt something going on. My body tensed and as I felt energy pouring into me, I began to feel it shooting out. A hard blast of light blinded me and I heard two bodies falling backwards. My vision returned quickly and I saw Jared and his friend getting up a few yards away and Ashley was racing for the door to the club. Jared bolted towards her, but I leapt forward and cut him off. I felt a surge of energy run up my arm and I clipped him good with a fist full of lightning. He fell back and then his friend came charging over. He was even bigger, somehow. His body looked like one big, overdeveloped muscle, but despite his size he was unusually agile. His body cut through the air like a knife and slammed me into the wall behind us with the force of a semi-truck. I was hoping he would have to step back and give me a moment to catch my breath, but instead he just started pounding me with his fists like a couple of jackhammers. My body tried to move, but I couldn't slip out between punches.

"Snake!" Jared barked. The punches stopped and I looked up as Snake stepped away and Jared came into view. "He gets excited easily. You see what Neon can do? You can't tell by looking at him now, but Snake there used to be a scrawny piece of nothin' once. A few shots of Neon and he blew up big time. I gotta say too, the ladies love the tongue." Jared said as Snake stuck his tongue out proudly.

"And you get to be Sparky, the wonder plug?" I said. Jared's eyes narrowed and he threw out his fist and a bolt of raw energy shot through me, knocking me back.

"The name's Volt! Smart mouth like that just earned you a little demonstration of how I can stop a heart with one touch." Jared said as he stooped to meet my eyes. His hand began to glow and spark with power and then he clutched at my chest. I felt his power surge through me again, but after a few seconds, it stopped. Volt kept his hand on me and I could feel the juice flowing through him, but it was like I was shielded.

I looked down at my arms and it was as though the suit was emitting an energy pulse that was absorbing Volt's power. I began to move and it seemed to throw Volt off guard. I quickly took advantage and pushed him back. I threw a few high powered punches and knocked him back to the ground. Snake came up behind me and locked his arms around me and began to squeeze. I tried to break free, but the pressure was growing far too intense. My arms were pinned to my sides and I couldn't concentrate. His pressure just steadily increased. I finally swung my legs back as hard as I could. It felt like kicking a steel wall. I did it again, but I soon realized I was probably doing more damage to myself.

I tried to concentrate harder and finally I felt a surge of energy grow within me. It began as a mere tingle and turned quickly into a torrent of power. I felt a fast rush push through my body and electricity started shooting out of every pore in my body. A flash of white light flooded my eyes but, despite my blindness, I heard a monstrous howl of pain and finally Snake's arms relaxed and I was free. Snake fell to the ground in a heap. I looked over and saw neither Volt nor Ashley were anywhere to be seen.

I searched the area and found a purse lying on the ground next to a nearby dumpster. I picked it up and quickly rifled through it. It was Ashley's. She must have dropped it in her haste to escape. I put it all back and quickly took off into the air just as a group of people came out from the club to find Snake lying unconscious.

12

I was at a slight loss as to what to do next, but then I realized I was obligated to return Ashley's purse. I thought maybe it was a little too mundane, but I chalked it up to one of those things that gets taken care of between the lines.

I checked her driver's license for her address. It was rather easy to locate. I had passed by her building several times that week. She lived in a small section of town not too far from the downtown city center. It was usually a very busy hub of activity as it was where most of the kids from the colleges lived and there usually was always some party going on, but as it was late, it seemed the natives were not all that restless for a change.

I was able to land right in front of her building. I noticed that most of the windows were dark. Considering the hour, that was not unusual. The sensible people of the world were fast asleep. I thought of retracting the suit and going in as myself. I would just pretend to be some good Samaritan returning a lost purse, but there were more questions I needed answers to, so I decided to figure a way in as Spectrum.

I flew back up and hovered along the side of the building, checking in on every window that was lit up. There weren't too many to choose from and there wasn't much going on in any of them. I lucked out and located Ashley's unit at the top floor.

She was sitting in her living room stooped over her laptop. I wasn't even sure if she was aware she had lost her bag. I noticed that her apartment had a balcony, so I landed on it and knocked gently on the glass. She looked up from her work and saw me immediately. She shook her head quickly, but then I held up her purse. She reluctantly got up and slid the door open for me.

"Lose something?" I asked as I tossed the bag into her waiting arms.

"Thanks. Good bye."

"Hold on. I think after what I saw, I earned some explanations. What the hell was all that?" I asked. Ashley looked to the floor and turned away from me. "What is going on here? Are you really researching for an article?" She quickly turned back to me.

"Yes. Everything I told you was true."

"Then what about Sparky? I sensed a little history there."

"Jared Pincer. He and I used to date," she said as she curled up behind her computer again.

"He was the guy you mentioned. The one who disappeared."

"Yes. I couldn't let anyone know we had been dating. My editor might have taken me off the story. We met at the office of the paper. Jared was just an assistant and I was starting as a features writer. He's the one who clued me in on the Neon thing. He would do most of the research and I'd put it together. It was great. I really got excited about the project. I felt like we were about to blow the lid off something huge, but then he disappeared. I didn't think much of it at first. He was always like that. Very mysterious. A free spirit. But I started to worry after I hadn't heard from him in almost two weeks. I looked around but no one knew anything. I started canvasing the hospitals and that's when I found him. He was the Jon Doe they had found unconscious in some back alley. He had been comatose since they found him and they didn't know who to contact. He woke up shortly after I found him but he couldn't tell me much. I got a hold of his blood work up and I could see the Neon in his blood had built up in his system and according to his doctor was the main reason for his condition. I told Jared about it but he wouldn't believe me. I went to see him the next day, but when I got to the hospital he was gone along with his files and his doctor. I asked around but no one could say anything. It was as though Jared had never been there. Every scrap of evidence of his existence was erased. I knew there was more going on and I knew I had to finish the piece. I had to expose Neon for the poison it was." I leaned against the wall taking in her story.

"What's the deal with Neon? How can it give people powers."

"I'm not sure, but from what little information I've gotten, it seems to act on a genetic level. DNA strands hold chromosomes that, over time, have become dormant. Either because of pollutants in our environment or just plain old, evolution, there are just some components of our genetic make up that aren't needed. Neon seems to latch onto the DNA and revives those dormant strands in receptive hosts. Ninety nine percent of the time, this results in the manifestation of abilities. I can only theorize that Jared's bio-electric field has been seriously upgraded. As for Snake, I assume the Neon plugged into the reptilian portion of his brain and took it from there."

"You seem to know quite a bit about this."

"I've been working this story for a long time. For a while, I was doing it for Jared."

"For a while?"

"I had to move on. That's when Sam entered the picture. He totally plugged into what I was doing and was ready to help from day one. I liked that. He could get into the clubs and press the contacts. We were so close to meeting the head of this operation. But, tonight." Ashley said but trailed off. "He was supposed to get a name from Spyder tonight." She began again with new resolve.

"I guess they were on to him."

"Probably. Hard to believe. We've been doing this for so long now. I would have thought if they smelled a rat, they would have come down on us long ago."

"This Neon business is that serious?"

"Yes. Neon is on the edge of being the next number one legal drug in America. This would be a catastrophe on several levels, which is why I'm trying to cut the beast off at the head now. Before it becomes an epidemic."

"I'd love to help you."

"Thanks, but without the info that Sam was supposed to get, I'm stuck," she said as she reached for her purse. She opened it up and pulled out a small phone. She looked down at it curiously. "Hmmm. Incoming." She clicked on her phone and the screen lit up. "Oh my god," she said with her eyes glued to the tiny screen.

"What?"

"Sam. It's an email from Sam. He must have sent this before..." She started, but stopped. Her focus was on whatever was on her screen. "He did it. He got it."

"A name?"

"Names and addresses. He got the mother lode! This is incredible!" she said as she frantically tapped away at her computer and her printer shot out a sheet of paper with a map and some directions printed on it. She grabbed it quickly and gazed at it as though it was the holy grail. She then quickly grabbed her purse and bolted for the door.

"Where are you going?"

"I have to follow up on this!"

"Now?"

"Yes! I can't let this wait any longer!" she said and rushed out the door. I spun around and leapt off her balcony and landed right in front of her building and intercepted her as she came out.

"Don't you think it's a little dangerous?"

"I don't care! I am so close to bringing this all to an end," she said as she pushed past me. I quickly snagged her arm and pulled her back.

"One more night won't make a difference. You need to rest and think about what you're doing." I urged. Suddenly, a bolt of electricity shot through the air and right into Ashley's apartment causing it to erupt in flame. I pulled her behind me to shield her.

"You were saying?" She asked.

"I'm new at this, okay?"

"They know where I live. They know where I work. My only leverage is finding out the truth behind their operation and until I find out, my life is in jeopardy," she said as she turned away and started toward a small car parked nearby. I ran up to her.

"You're not going alone."

"Okay. Fine. Get in," she said as she held the door to her car open.

"In that?"

"Of course. I have the directions here. I can take us right to the heart of the operation."

"That's great, but, I can fly. You know?" She looked at me blankly.

"So?"

"I don't need to ride in the car. I can fly. I'll follow."

"You'll follow my car from way up there?"

"Yes." Her eyes glazed over.

"That doesn't make any sense! Just get in the damn car!"

Moments later, I was fidgeting in the seat next to Ashley as she piloted her car along the highway.

"You need the air conditioner?"

"No. I'm fine. Thanks."

"You don't seem fine."

"This is weird. I feel weird."

"But you'd feel more comfortable floating miles above all this?"

"I just feel a little awkward." I said as I felt my suit sliding against the vinyl seat.

"You could just take it off, or tear it off, or whatever you do with that thing."

"I can't just take it off right in front of you!"

"Please! Unless you're really Brad Pitt under that thing, I doubt

I'd ever know who you really are, with or without the costume."

"It's not that."

"Then what?"

"I'm naked under this."

"Really?"

"Well, I've got my underwear, but still."

"Cute. You're shy."

"Again, I'm new at this. I haven't really worked with anyone else like this."

"Okay. Fine. If you really want to fly, just open the door and hop out." She suggested.

"No, it's fine." I said as I propped my head up and looked out the window.

The trip through the city was quiet. Ashley took mostly back streets and avoided any major veins of activity. Once we crossed over the bay bridge, it felt as though we had fallen off the edge of the world. There were very few cars on the road and there was nothing but darkness surrounding us.

"So." Ashley said suddenly. "I'm sure you get asked this a lot, but I can't in good conscience let this opportunity pass without joining in. Why do you do this?"

"Do what?"

"The hero thing. Busting up the muggers and crackpots. I've kept up with what you've been doing. Why do you do it?"

"I guess I never really thought about it before, but the best I can offer you is I felt it was the right thing to do at first."

"At first?"

"Yeah. After I put out a few fires, I started to feel something I haven't felt in a long time. I felt like I was worth something. I felt like I was contributing to the world and I haven't ever felt like that before this."

"So, you're entire motivation to be this altruistic hero was a completely selfish need to validate your own ego."

"Well, I think I prefer my phrasing."

"I'm sorry. I don't mean anything by that. I mean, if it takes something that just makes you feel good to do something good for everyone else, that's fine. At least you're doing something positive. It's a lot more than most people can say."

"Thanks. I think."

We were well out of the city. It looked like nothing but darkness beyond the asphalt, except for a few clusters of dotted lights far out in the distance. They looked like little gated communities peppered along the wide open spaces of the undeveloped lands that surrounded Towers City.

It was a stark contrast to the bustling big city that the world saw it as. I cracked the window open and the distinct aroma of sea air shot in and I felt the brace of the ice cold wind. The radio played in the background, but my attention was focused outside. I had always been fascinated by what could not be seen at night. I flashed on moments from my youth when we'd go out to dinner and come driving back home long after the sun had gone down. While mom and dad talked in the front seat, I'd have my eyes on the growing darkness outside. My mind would wonder and fantasize about what mysteries were lurking right there in plain sight. The darkness seemed boundless and unending to me then. It felt as though I could just reach out and risk falling into it forever. It scared me and intrigued me equally.

Finally, the car came to a turn off and we rode off the paved road and onto a dirt one. We tumbled along when finally Ashley pulled over and consulted her phone.

"Well?"

"Just a minute. The signal's in and out in these parts. My kingdom for a tower."

"Where are we now?"

"I don't know. I think this is some old utility road. There are lots of them out here. The farms just outside of town use them."

"Farms?"

"Sure. You don't think that milk just appears on your table in the morning, do you?"

"I just didn't know there were any farms anywhere near Towers."

"You are new in town."

"Well, if you know where we are, why are we stopped?"

"These utility roads connect around like mazes. One wrong turn and we could be lost for hours. I'm just trying to get a fix on where we need to go," she said as she gazed at her phone with careful eyes. Her eyes lit up suddenly and she popped up in her seat. "There!" She quickly turned the car back on and we proceeded down the road.

The only light to be had was from the headlights of the car. The further we got, the less I could smell the sea air and the more it began to smell exactly the way I imagined a farm would smell, so I rolled the windows back up fast. The ride seemed to get bumpier with each turn and I could see the dust kicking up in a thick cloud all around us. The car began to slow and we were stopped in front of a white metal gate. It looked old and rusted. The paint was worn in many places and I could see signs of rust on the hinges from where I was sitting.

"This is it," she said as she looked forward, past the gate. On the other side, the road continued on into darkness. Ashley reached for her buckle, but before she could, I waved my hand and a hum of power filled the air. As quickly as that, the gate sprung open right in front of us. She looked over to me. Her expression was hard to misinterpret.

"Impressive. I admit." She started the car up again.

13

After we passed through the gate, Ashley switched off the lights and we continued through the cover of darkness. And it was dark. There were no lights anywhere around. The road was smoother though. She drove slowly and I could hear the faint sound of tires rolling over thick grass outside. We finally reached the end of the path and the light of the moon above exposed what lay before us. A large industrial looking complex. One large main building in the middle with a couple of smaller buildings built around it. One of them looked like a storage facility. The barn. The main building looked more like a science center than a farmhouse. Two large towers stood over it and there didn't appear to be any windows.

"It looks abandoned."

"These are the directions I had, and this is where they led me."

"Doesn't look like anyone's home."

"There's got to be something here."

"Let me check." She looked to me, but before she could utter a single objection I pushed my hand to her mouth. "I'll just take a quick look and then, if it's safe, you can come in." I said as I opened the car door and lifted out. I stepped away from the car and got a better look at the whole complex. I pushed off and flew high over the field and drifted over to the buildings.

I landed on the roof of the large central complex which seemed to be the heart of the operation. There were some skylights and I peered inside. I saw several large vats inside filled with glowing fluids. They were being churned and mixed steadily. I still couldn't see anyone around. It seemed to be an automated operation. I walked along the side of the roof until I came upon a door which I assumed would lead me inside. I sent a charge through the lock and heard something release. I pulled the door open. It revealed a long corridor leading down. There were pipes and wires all over the place but they all seemed to be leading to the same destination, but before I could walk in, a piercing siren whined in the air and lights came on all around me. I jumped back and charged myself up, ready for anything, but I saw all the attention was further away. I ran to the other edge of the building and I could see Ashley running away, followed by two large uniformed guards. I was about to jump up and go after her, but before I could act, the guards had already snagged her. I crouched back into the darkness as they brought her back towards the building. I hurried through the open door as quietly as I could.

I walked down and found myself in a maze of tubes and lights. It looked as though someone had gutted the whole building and rebuilt it on the inside only. The floor looked like some kind of metal and the fixtures looked as though someone had spent a lifetime planning on their placement. I searched through every dark tunnel I came across, trying to find some path toward anything. I was getting to the point I didn't care if I walked in on a firing squad armed to the teeth, I just wanted to see another human being.

I finally discovered a large pipe that looked rather essential, so I followed it and it took me to a small pathway that led me onto a small catwalk above the main floor with all the vats. There were pipes coming from everywhere, dumping all kinds of weird liquids into all the vats. I thought they were glowing brightly outside, but they were at least three times that bright in person. I was nearly blinded until I was startled by the sound of a door being pushed open. I slid into a dark corner and I saw the guards from outside burst in with Ashley in tow. They stopped suddenly and another figure appeared, seemingly from out of nowhere. It looked to be a man. A very slender man with an odd body and wearing a top hat.

"I understand you were interested in a tour." The odd man said.

"You're making poison."

"Yes. I know. I really don't like it when people feel compelled to point out the obvious."

"You can't think that you can just keep doing this!"

"I actually do. I've been doing this for quite a while already."

"You're killing innocent people!" Ashley begged. The odd man bent down and took her chin between his long fingers.

"Those are usually the most satisfying, I admit. I don't know why. I guess it's because they just don't expect it as much, you know? They're never ready. I wonder who it was in their lives that told them that the innocent are immune from punishment. In my experience, they're the first draft picks. To that end, I believe some friends of yours have come to say hello. I'll leave you to your socializing," he said and soon I saw Volt and Snake come in and join them just as the guy in the top hat turned to leave. As he did so, I thought I saw him look up directly at me. My heart froze for a moment, but he just walked away, back into the darkness. I crawled along the catwalk closer to Ashley. Volt and Snake were closing in on her.

"You shouldn't have come here." Volt said.

"I had to. I had to know why you've done this to yourself. Is all of this worth it?"

"I have orders to kill you."

"What's stopping you?"

"I don't want to do this to you, Ash. I just wish you could see it from here."

"All I see is a pathetic loser who got sucked into this nightmare and now you're hopped up on this trash. You were weak," she said. Volt turned away from her and tensed. His arm flew out and a bolt blasted out from his fist and caused a small explosion against the wall. He spun around quickly.

"I am not weak! I am strong! Before, I was weak, but then I had a taste of real power and I wised up. I was on the wrong side of the fence the whole time. Now I've seen the light. Neon is a miracle. It has led me to be who I was meant to be."

"An electricity spewing psycho?"

"This is just the beginning, Ash. Snake and me? All the others using Neon? We are the first generation of a new level of human evolution. Neon has brought us millions of years forward in terms of human physical growth. We may be freaks to you now, but in time, we'll be the norm. This is what humanity is heading towards. We see that. Why can't you?"

"I don't care what you call this! Neon is toxic! It's killing people!"

"It's not killing me. In fact, I don't even use the stuff anymore."

"What about the people who need to use Neon to keep their powers going? They need fixes on a daily basis just to stay normal. People are dying."

"Those are the weak ones and they might as well just die off now. They are not worthy of the future that is in store for us all. Ash, it's not too late for you."

"What do you mean?" She asked. Volt reached into his pocket and pulled out a vial that glowed white in the darkness.

"The boss gave this to me. He says this is the purest form of Neon in the world. One sip and you're a god." Volt said. He pulled the top off and approached Ashley. She began to back away. "Snake." Volt said. Snake then raced forward and grabbed Ashley. Volt got closer to her and was about to force the drug into her mouth, but I leapt over the railing and landed flat on the floor. I fired two bolts of energy at them. I managed to knock Volt back but Snake just tossed Ashley aside and charged toward me. I clamped onto his shoulders as he rammed into me and flipped him over, throwing him back against one of the vats. I turned back to Ashley and saw Volt pouring the white liquid into her mouth and then she passed out in his arms. I lunged at him, but it was too late. Ashley came awake quickly and started coughing violently. I grabbed Volt and punched him hard across his face, but he only smiled in deep satisfaction. I punched him again and again. His face was covered in blood, but he was still so damn smug.

"It's too late, hero," I turned and saw Ashley standing still, her head down. I walked over to her, but she looked at me suddenly. Her eyes were bursting with light and suddenly there was light everywhere. Ashley floated up above the floor and bolts of pure energy were pouring down around her. I didn't know what was happening and it didn't seem she did either. She came back down to the ground and Volt ran to her. "You see now? What you're feeling now, I feel all the time! This is the way, Ash. You know I'm right," he said, but suddenly her head whipped up and a blast of white light shot from her eyes, knocking Volt back. Snake lumbered toward her, but she blasted him just as easily. I approached Ashley but as her eyes turned to me, I leapt up, and her blast missed me completely. Instead, it hit one of the vats, causing a flood of purple liquid to pour out. She turned and fired another shot breaking another vat which released a yellow liquid. Volt and Snake were racing out of the building in a panic.

"Ashley! Stop!"

"I can't!" she said in a pained tone. "Get out of here!"

"Just calm down! Breathe!"

"No. I can end this. I can end this all right now!" she said and began firing more energy out of her eyes. The walls were shaking and fires were exploding out everywhere. I tried to reach Ashley, but she rose up into the air and with one continuous beam, she ignited all of the remaining chemical vats. I got out as fast as I could.

I found my way out of the building just as it started to come apart at the seams. I tried to get as far as I could but before I could get clear the whole building exploded in an eruption of fire and debris. The force of the blast pushed me forward and I skidded along the rough ground.

The Earth beneath us began to crack and weaken and the other buildings began to sink into a deep, dark hole. I watched as the last bit of smoke billowed up from the crater that was left behind. I was about to walk away when I saw a small arm reach up out of the hole. I raced over and pulled Ashley up. Her skin was pale and her breathing labored.

"It's gone. I destroyed it all," she said in a dream like tone.

"I'm getting you to a doctor." I said.

"No. They can't help me. Not now, but it's okay. I did what I needed to do. I did what the world needed me to do."

"That's great, but I wasn't asking if you wanted to see a doctor. We're going now." I said, but as I lifted her up, I could feel the weight of her body. Her skin was already growing cold. I looked down at her face and her eyes were closed and the peace in her face was unmistakable. I set her back down on the ground gently.

"She was a good girl." Volt said from behind. I spun around and charged some energy into my fist. He lifted his hand at me quickly. "Put it away, dude. Fight's over," he said as he walked over to Ashley's body. "I never thought it would go this far. She wasn't supposed to find out about any of this. I guess I should have known she would have, though. She's like that."

"You still cared about her?"

"Of course. I've changed a lot because of Neon, but some things just don't go away that easily. I wanted her away from this because I didn't want her to get hurt. Goes to show you how well plans work out, huh?"

"She had moved on."

"With Sam? I know. I think that's why I fried him. I didn't really have to, but in the back of my head I hated him for taking her from me."

"You let her go." I said. Volt stood up over Ashley's body.

"That's what I thought at first. We fool ourselves like that. We love someone for so long and we say we let them go, but that's just a lie. They never leave us. We're trapped by them. Someone told me that love takes no prisoners. Seems to me, that's all love does. We're all held by it. Either by choice or design. There's no escape," he said and then turned away and walked back toward the road. I jumped forward and grabbed his arm.

"Not so fast. This isn't over yet."

"For me it is." Volt said and he quickly grabbed my arm and sent a jolt of energy right through me. I fell back with a sharp ringing in my ears. "Sorry, man. I just can't deal with this right now, but I'll do you a favor. I'll give you the name of the guy who's really in charge. Crazy dude calling himself Sur Reel. He's the guy who brought in the Neon in the first place. His own recipe, or so he told me. Feel free to go after him, and maybe later we can pick up this dance where we left off. Until then, ciao!" Volt said and ran off. I let my head fall back and everything grew dark.

It felt like hours had passed as I woke up, but it had only been a few minutes. Ashley's body still laid silent and Volt and Snake were nowhere to be seen. I heard the sound of a helicopter approaching and the sirens of some emergency vehicles getting closer. I bid Ashley one last farewell and took off into the night sky.

I watched from the top of a nearby hill as the police swarmed in over the area. They found Ashley and loaded her up and sped away. For a moment, I saw something of interest and almost as if by command, the suit allowed my eyes to focus more closely. It was like having a telescope in my head. As my eyes adjusted, I could see one of the police officers on the scene was Tyler. It felt like ages since I had seen him last. My heart fluttered a bit at the sight of his face. Then Volt's words echoed in my head. I turned away and headed back towards Towers City.

14

I woke up the next morning feeling heavier in my heart. I had never actually seen anyone die before. I could feel the life slip out of Ashley as I held her in my arms. She felt so limp and heavy. Her eyes were glassy and soulless. The whole night felt like some kind of twisted nightmare. I was just glad it was over at last.

As I padded to the sofa, my thoughts drifted to giving up the hero thing before it was too late. One dead body was bad enough. I couldn't help but think there could be more if I insisted on continuing this crusade. I flipped on the TV and the news was on. I came on in the middle of the story, but it was about Neon. They were talking about the discovery of the lab and how the police were going to take a serious look at the growing Neon issue. I turned to another channel and there was more of the same. Chief Kelvin was scheduled for a press conference later to address the incident from the other night in particular. Fortunately, there was no mention of Spectrum. I shut the TV off, and I began to feel a bit better. She did what she set out to do. Ashley wanted to expose the Neon market, and she did it. Everyone was talking about it. Of course, it could mean those who are amped on the drug may feel there's no need to stay hidden any longer. It could lead to a new wave of crime in the city, but I didn't want to dwell on that. A little measure of good was done in the world, and that much made me smile.

I stepped out into the hall and was caught by Heather's gaze as she stepped out at the same time.

"Cosmic," she said. "Do you have any idea what the odds of you and I walking out into this hall at the exact same time, at this time of day are? I think you'd be surprised by the answer."

"Morning, Heather."

"Don't you mean good morning?"

"Is it good?"

"We're alive, right? Makes it good enough."

"Okay. Sure."

"Someone doesn't sound very happy."

"It's just one of those days, okay?"

"Fine. Enough said. You headed out to work?"

"Unfortunately, yes. Another three hour shift."

"Oh, by the way, I talked to the owner to the building about your rent situation, and he said it was okay."

"You're kidding!"

"Actually, yes. He was quite pissed, but I finessed him pretty good. I think it'll be okay."

"You didn't have to sleep with him, did you?"

"Jason. You're a cool guy and all, but not even for my mother would I take that bullet. No, I just said I'd cover what you couldn't."

"Heather! What? No!"

"Why not? I can afford it. That trust fund of mine is really awesome."

"I don't know what to say. Thank you."

"No problem. I just get this feeling about you."

"What feeling?" I asked. Heather regarded me oddly and walked up to me. She put her palms flat on the sides of my face.

"I don't know. You just look like one of those guys who works real hard, but no one notices or cares. I figure, a guy like that deserves at least one break, right?"

"Yeah." I said, but my voice stuttered a bit as I became a little emotional before I could stop it.

"Go on to work. I'll hold down the fort here," she said with a smile. I nodded to her and quickly headed for the stairs.

I thought on Heather's generosity as I fought my way to work. I promised myself she would not have to support me for long. Support me. She hardly knew me, and she so readily accepted the task of covering my rent. I had never in my life known anyone so kind and generous. I felt tears well up behind my eyes a couple times along my commute. They disappeared quickly as I approached the cafe.

I saw Tyler and Dave standing outside in their full uniforms. I felt something cold in my stomach as I walked up to them. I did my best to smile.

"Hey, Jason!" Dave said as he took my hand in his. His grip was tight and sweaty.

"Hi, Dave. Tyler. What's all this?"

"We were just heading out. We're on detail for Kelvin's press conference."

"Oh. Okay. Is it some big deal?"

"Kind of. Everyone's afraid some Neon freaks may show up and cause trouble. After what happened last night, I wouldn't be surprised if they did." Dave added.

"Why's that? They're exposed now. Right?"

"It's like disturbing a hornet's nest. You poke it, they come out to sting. It's all just a precaution. I'm sure it'll be fine,"

"All right. Be careful." I caught Dave's eye suddenly. "Both of you."

"Yeah. Sure. See ya." Dave said brusquely and soon he grabbed Tyler's arm and they hurried away. I let out a breath and pushed through the doors into the cafe.

I saw Bethany at the counter talking to Tristan. His eyes were rolling at a rate of once per every two words, so I bypassed him and went on to slip on my apron. I walked back out and started sweeping the floor, as there weren't any patrons to deal with yet.

"Let's ask an objective party." I heard Bethany say. I felt her eyes find me and soon she was up and dragging me to the counter. I looked at her and there was a kind of slip in reality. I had never been so close to anyone I had seen on television. It was like she jumped out of the tube and right into my face. "My brother and I were discussing my career options. He says that I'm not hard news material, but I say that I am. What do you think?" She asked. Her words settled on my brain. Whenever I saw Bethany on TV, she was talking celebrity gossip or on some local infomercial. I think the closest I had seen her do news was when she filled in for the weather girl for a week during hurricane season. "I ask not as your employer and the person who holds your life, and future, in her hands, but as a serious news person."

"Yeah, no pressure." Tristan said.

"Serious news? Like wars and stuff?" I asked.

"Yes. Can't you see me as the next Diane Sawyer?" I looked over to Tristan who threw up his hands in surrender and turned away quickly. I looked back to Bethany. I still hadn't said anything. I could feel the sweat on my brow growing.

"Sure." I said at last. Tristan ran back and looked me right in the face. I stared him back just as quickly.

"Really?" She chirped.

"Really?" he said in utter astonishment.

"Yes. I think if you have the drive and passion to be or do something, you can do it. I think Bethany can do the news."

"The woman who thought The Hague was a special kind of sandwich? Serious news?"

"You heard the man!" Bethany said proudly. "That's why I should be at that press conference today!"

"You wanted to cover it?" I asked.

"Well, of course! It's history! First we get a super hero, now we've got lots of little super powered freaks running around town. It's exciting!"

"Exciting?" Tristan said sharply.

"Yes. Up until now this town has been so boring. We are witnessing history in the making."

"Tell me that after you get attacked by one of those freaks!" Tristan shot back. "I know it's all fun to think about in theory, but when you live with all this strangeness, it's a completely different story."

"It's exciting. It's the dawning of a new age for everyone. Who knows what else could happen? Maybe we'll make contact with visitors from space!"

"I think you should make contact with a psychiatrist."

"Jason believes. Don't you?" She asked, turning her head to me.

"I guess. I mean, there's a lot we don't know about the universe. I suppose anything is possible."

"Anything is possible! Thank you! That's it exactly." Bethany said enthusiastically and then turned back to Tristan. "Why can't you have that kind of faith? Why do you have to see everything in black and white?"

"Because, sister dear, that's the way of the world. The real way of the world. Now, if Jason is quite done sucking up, there are some cups that need rinsing in the kitchen."

"Yes, sir." I said and hurried into the back as quickly as I could.

I discovered a mountain of dirty coffee cups in the sink and began the task of washing them which took me a little more than an hour and for all that time, I could hear only the sound of Tristan and Bethany argue. It wasn't hard to see that they were indeed related.

After a prolonged silence, I heard the bell on the front door ring. I peered out and saw Bethany had gone.

"Is it safe?" Tristan looked over at me and smiled.

"Yeah. Coast is clear." I stepped out and sat at the counter where Bethany had been moments earlier.

"She's something."

"Yeah. Don't get me wrong. She's my sister and I love her, but there are times I just want to rip every last strand of hair out of her skull."

"I never had any siblings."

"Count yourself lucky."

"Where did she go?"

"To the press conference. She figures if she can't be there as a reporter, she can be there as a spectator."

"She really likes news."

"She likes being the center of attention. She's always been like that. I'm sure she'll figure some way to get that microphone into her hands."

The rest of my shift went on as usual. A few cups poured here and a few muffins served there. I looked up and saw that it was just a few minutes shy of eleven. I turned to put my apron away, but Tristan came out and flipped on the television over the counter.

"Show time."

"The press conference?"

"Bingo. Let's see if sis can pull off the American dream," he said as the feed appeared on the screen. It looked to be a live remote in front of city hall. There was a podium set up and reporters were flanked on either side. The state flag was set on one side and the city flag on the other. Four police guards were lined behind the podium. I saw that one of them was Tyler. He looked so handsome in his uniform. His posture was firm and proud. His chest was puffed out. I could tell he was pushing it out more than he normally does. Tyler was never the type to let his emotions show too easily but it was clear he was more excited than he would ever admit.

I saw Kelvin come on after a few minutes. He looked just like I thought an old cop would look. He had close cropped black hair and a firm, thick build. His face seemed to be in a constant sneer. His brows inclined over his nose and gave him an angry kind of appearance.

"Ladies and gentlemen. I realize that after the events that occurred at the abandoned Davidson Dairy farm last night, there have been a lot of wild stories flying around. Some have been saying we're being overrun by a race of superhuman freaks. That simply is not true. The facts we have as of now tell us that Neon is indeed connected to the manifestation of powers in some individuals. We have not finished our research of the drug in question, but I would like to announce now that, thanks to some fast action by our representatives in the capital, possession or use of the drug Neon is set to be illegal very soon. I am setting up task forces specifically to deal with this new, emerging problem," he said. Kelvin just kept droning on and on, but my eyes couldn't leave Tyler. His eyes were sparkling like I had never seen before. I could see then that his life in Towers City was a lot different than his life in Blue Haven. He would never had found this honor back in Blue Haven. He was a lot different in Towers than he was at home.

In a perfect world, I wouldn't be as in love with the new Tyler as I was the old, but it wasn't and I couldn't stop loving him, but too much had changed in his life and I had to start changing my own.

15

The advent of the Neon threat changed a lot in Towers City, but I had a feeling Neon was just an excuse to beef up the manhunt for Spectrum. Neon incidents were few and far between even with the truth of the effects of the drug leaking out, yet measures for security were tripled. In fact, Manicore Industries was the first to step up and offer corporate sponsorship. Manicore went so far as to unveil a new brand of security force to the Towers City police department. Drone Droids.

The press release said that these humanoid robots were the most advanced example of the fusion between robotics and artificial intelligence. They were fully loaded with cutting edge laser weapons, which I was unable to defend myself against since they were also energy based, as well as micro-missiles and surveillance equipment. They could fly and track any living thing. They said they would be deployed gradually over the year until there were at least sixty on patrol at a single time.

The police and a Manicore representative said they were being used to suppress the threat of any Neo-Human activity, but it seemed their true main objective was to bring my head in on a silver platter.

Where I was, they were. It seemed I couldn't fly around anywhere in the city without attracting the attention of two or three of the jolly mechanical men. Once, they bypassed a Neo-Human incident in favor of tracking me down for over an hour. It seemed to me Manicore had more of a bone to pick with me than anyone else, but I had no idea why.

I was feeling particularly restless and felt an irresistible need to go out. It was as though the suit inside me was screaming at me. Begging me to take it out, so I relented. I slipped out through my skylight, as usual, and just flew. I didn't know where I wanted to go and I didn't really care. When I flew, it was as though the world and everything in it disappeared. My crippling debt and lack of income vanished from my mind. My anxieties about being the most hunted man in the city faded just as easily. Then I thought of Tyler, and despite my elation as I soared effortlessly through the night sky, he brought me back to Earth. I didn't want to think about him. I tried like Hell to keep him out of my thoughts, but I couldn't help myself. I couldn't control it.

Before I realized it, I was far over the city center. I looked down. The dazzling lights and shimmering hues of the city at night were like a galaxy of stars below me. I swooped down a bit until I could hear the faint sounds of the traffic. I couldn't believe this had become normal for me, but it had. I took a deep breath and since I had not encountered any kind of disruption, I felt it was time to start heading back home but as I was turning, I saw a small armada of Drone Droids flying up toward me.

As they got closer, I saw a few of them raise their arms and small gun turrets popped out of their forearms and began firing laser blasts at me. I shot up higher, but they shot up right behind me. Their firing increased in frequency and the air was starting to get thin, so I decided to take the fight down to them. I dropped down and slipped past them easily, which confused them and as they reconfigured their guidance systems, I put as much mileage between them and me as I could.

After I thought I had finally shaken them, another swarm of tin men cropped up. I turned and saw another platoon approaching. I hadn't seen so many out at night at once. I shot down like a bullet, and they were right behind me as I did. The closer to the ground I got, the faster they got. Once I landed, I heard them come down onto the ground with a chorus of metallic thuds. I looked over and saw a small army of robots all aiming their arm guns at me. My mind was racing. I had to admit to a little fear. The Drone Droids seemed like a joke to me at first, but when you've got twenty or so of those killing machines staring you down, the joke doesn't seem as funny anymore.

As if by reflex, I swung my arm around and unleashed a large wave of electric energy. It seemed to knock them back a bit, but they were still standing. I threw out a more concentrated beam of energy, which blasted a hole through the torso of one Drone Droid, but the others continued to advance on me. It seemed a few were trying to fire their weapons, but I guess my first strike knocked out their weapons systems. I took the opportunity and charged forward. I dove into them thrashing away. The suit cushioned my hands, so punching them felt no worse than punching my pillow. I heard the hollow crunch of metal as I landed blow after blow. It felt as though I had torn through most of the Drones, but as I turned, I saw another batch arriving on the scene. A sharp pain stabbed me at the base of my neck and something in my body let go. I turned to one of the fallen droids and held my arm out to it. Soon, my arm began to shake and shimmer with energy. The scrap metal leapt up and absorbed into my arm. After the suit had soaked up all the metal it could, my hands began to grow. My fingers grew longer and came to very sharp points, like claws. A surge of energy took me over. It was like a thousand jolts right into my brain. Like my body was filling with energy and it had to be released somehow.

I looked over at the advancing party of rust buckets and something primal in me took over. I dove into them and started slashing away wildly. I tore their arms off and ripped through their midsections. Parts and gears with wires attached were flying everywhere.

My body was moving as though I were being controlled by something else. My arms swung back and forth seamlessly as I cut a swath through the blockade of Drone Droids. I felt almost like I was underwater, every movement thought out and with purpose, but I was moving so much faster. Like some kind of ballet set on fast forward. I had never felt such a rush of adrenaline in my life.

Before I realized it, I had mowed down every last one of them. I stood over the strewn debris of the fallen robots. My breathing was deep and full. I looked down at my handiwork. My fingers shrank back down to normal as the suit calmed down. My body was humming with torrents of power. I could hear sirens in the distance and decided it was a good idea to leave, so I bolted.

As I returned home, I felt a twinge in my side. I looked down and saw a bloody cut across my abdomen. I guess one of the robots got lucky. I hadn't even felt it though.

I dropped to the street and walked into the building. I didn't think I could take anymore flying. It was late so I was confident I could make it to my door without being spotted.

As I got to my unit and pushed the door open, I heard the door behind me open. I turned and saw Heather standing across from me with her arms folded over each other. I felt like my brain had checked out in that instant.

"Hi." I said. Heather just stood there. Silent. A small crack of a smile grew across her lips.

"I knew it!" she said as she skipped over to me.

"What do you mean you knew it?"

"You really think a superhero is going to live across the hall from me and I won't figure it out? Come inside," she said as she led me back into her place. She shut the door and quickly retrieved her laptop and called up some kind of chart on it.

"What's all that?"

"It's a chart of all the electrical activity in the building. I started keeping an eye on it back when I found the DWP padding my bill. Look at this," she said as she clicked on a particular chart. "This was the reading I got the night that kid got attacked outside and the readings have been holding at this level ever since. And it's not coming from the building."

"It could have been."

"Really? You're standing in front of me in that and still trying to deny?"

"Okay. Fine. I'm busted. What are you going to do now? Turn me in?"

"Are you crazy? I would never do that. Although, getting an inside look at what that suit can do would be a nice way to pay me back for keeping a big secret."

"I wish I could, but I don't know much about this thing myself. Seems like every day I learn something new. I just found out I can absorb metal and use it to augment the suit."

"Really?"

"Yeah. I trashed a platoon of Drone Droids."

"Well, what do you know about it?"

"Its powers seem to be energy based. Electricity. Light. Magnetism. I can fly. It makes me stronger. Works out my body."

"But how does it work? Is it alien? Man made?"

"I don't know."

"What do you mean you don't know?"

"I don't know! I got injected with this thing in some back alley science experiment. I don't know where it came from or what it is."

"I have to study it. I can't pass this up. May I have a sample?"

"Sure, but how are you going to study it?"

"My dad is a big wig at the R & D department at Manicore. He lets me use his lab all the time. Hold still," she said as she grabbed a sharp looking knife. She reached for my leg and pulled a small bit of the suit out. Just before she was about to cut it off, it pulled back. "Whoa."

"You must have lost grip."

"No. It pulled back. This thing is alive."

"That's impossible. Are you sure it just didn't slip?"

"I swear! It pulled away!"

"It would explain a lot."

"Let me try again." She took another bit of the costume and as she tried to cut it, it pulled away again. "This isn't going to work. You're going to have to come into the lab. That's the only way."

"I don't know."

"Don't you want some answers? I mean, a living thing of indeterminate origin is attached to your body. Doesn't that freak you out?"

"Well, when you say it like that..."

"Trust me. It won't hurt. I'll go in easy. We can do it after business hours so no one will know. I promise." She pleaded.

"Fine." I said at last.

16

The next day I went down to Manicore's main headquarters downtown with Heather. She had her father's security pass and since the guard at the front desk recognized her, he waved us through with no problem.

Manicore's headquarters' lobby was very off putting. The walls were cold marble and everywhere you turned there were paintings and statues of dragons. There was also a large golden Manicore logo embedded in the outside facing wall that overlooked the entire lobby. It looked like a dragon's head with the name Manicore spelled just below it.

We got to the elevators and went up to the twentieth floor.

"Seems kind of cold."

"Welcome to corporate America. Manicore isn't big on warm and cuddly."

"And your dad works here?"

"He's mostly just a consultant. He doesn't even really need the money. He just likes to stay in the game."

"You didn't tell him why we were doing this, did you?"

"Relax. Like I said, I do this all the time."

"Why do you bother? You've got a full lab right in your living room."

"Wait until you see what they've got here. It's nerd paradise," she said. I could tell she was growing excited. The closer we got to our destination, the more she started to bounce on the balls of her feet. She even started to hum a bit.

The elevator came to a stop and the doors slid open and I saw what she was talking about. The lab must have taken up the entire floor. From the threshold of the elevator and on, it was all high tech lab. Computer stations lined across the walls. All kinds of high tech junk was laid out everywhere. It looked like what I always thought the inside of an alien starship would look like. Heather ran ahead of me and danced around like she was a child at Disneyland. She did a quick spin and took a deep breath.

"I love the smell of a lab. Come on. Let's kick out some science!" she said. She went straight to work at one of the nearby computer terminals but I chose to explore around a bit.

There wasn't too much to see. Everything looked very technical and way over my head. There were a few research projects on the floor that looked to be unfinished, but I didn't know what they were for. I then came upon a section that had what appeared to be a second generation Drone Droid. It was a bit bigger than the ones they were already making and the design looked more streamlined and lean. Something to look forward to.

"I'm ready for you!" Heather called out. I hurried over to her and saw that she had a whole little section all laid out for the examination. There was a large table for me to sit on and she had several non-threatening pieces of equipment and some surgical tools that also looked minimally hazardous sitting on a nearby table. She looked up at me as I approached. "Okay. Suit on." She instructed. I closed my eyes and I felt the suit envelope me quickly and I looked back at Heather. She had a rather impressed expression on her face. "That was pretty cool. Now hop on," she said as she patted the table. I sat down and she flipped on her equipment. "The party begins now."

It took almost an hour. Heather worked quickly, but silently as she examined and inspected every inch of me that I would allow her access to. She was like an experienced surgeon as she worked. Totally focused on the task. She took some base readings of my body. She attached wires and sensors to my arms and legs and checked my blood pressure. It all seemed rather routine. I tried to read her face to gauge what she was discovering but she was unreadable and that worried me.

She concluded the test by clamping down a section of the suit and cutting it off. As she did, a shock of pain raced through me. It wasn't unbearable, but it was deep. The suit seemed to rally quickly enough though. I watched as Heather put the sample into a small glass vial.

"Well?" I asked as I pulled the wires and pads from me.

"I didn't find out much yet but this sample will fill in a lot of blanks."

"How long is that going to take?"

"I don't know. This thing is clearly a very complex organism. I also have to do this very quietly. We can't risk this raising any red flags."

"I suppose not."

"You do realize if anyone finds out about this, we could be arrested, right? Well, I'd be arrested. You'd probably get sealed away in some government lab."

"Well, this whole thing was your idea, remember?"

"I just want to make sure you understand the risks. I'll get these tests done as quickly as possible."

"So, we're done here?" I asked.

"Yeah. We're done. Let me just clean all this up and we can get out of here."

Later that evening, I felt too tired from the examination to bother with going on patrol, but I was also too restless to just sit at home so I decided to take a walk.

One of the benefits of flying around the city as Spectrum was being able to familiarize myself with the various streets and neighborhoods within it. There were so many that it would take the average person decades to uncover them all, but shooting through the air as I did, I was able to map them out and discover little nooks and crannies that I would otherwise never know about.

I trailed along a nearby boulevard a few blocks away from my building. I just walked and walked for blocks. I lost myself in my thoughts. My phone jostled me from my trance as it rang out.

"Hello?"

"Hello, sweety!" My mother chirped.

"Hi, mom; what's going on?"

"Nothing, I just wanted to check in. It's been so long since your father or I have heard from you," she said in a less than subtle tone.

"Sorry."

"It's fine. You're probably very busy. So, tell me. What's going on?"

"Nothing really new to report. I'm still at the coffee house."

"Oh."

"What?"

"Nothing,"

"Your tone sounded a bit disappointed."

"No, honey. We couldn't be prouder of you."

"But,"

"I'm just worried. How is working in that diner going to secure your future? You're not going to be young forever."

"I realize that, mom, but it takes time."

"How about school? You have your Associate's from the community college here. I'm sure you could take some night courses and get your Bachelor's."

"I have considered that, but I can't afford the tuition right now."

"There's always financial aid...." She continued.

"Mom! Please. I get it. You're worried. I appreciate it, but I'm just not in the mood to talk about this right now."

"What does that matter? Are you all right? Do you need money?"

"No. I just have some stuff on my mind. I've actually taken on a second job."

"Really?" She asked. Her tone went up drastically. "What kind of work is it?"

"It's more of a volunteer position."

"Oh." Her mood fell.

"But it's very fulfilling. I think it could turn into something big for me."

"I hope so," she said. I felt the motherly concern seep through the phone and wrap around me like a warm, gentle hug. I looked up for a moment and saw a small diner a block away. I had seen it several times before and had always wanted to go in to try it out, but never found the time. I decided that the conditions were right and after everything I had been through, I deserved a treat.

I headed towards it as my mother continued talking into my ear. When I got close enough, my heart stopped. I could see Tyler sitting in a booth inside. Alone and not in uniform. My heart skipped a few beats ahead in a second and I froze in my place. I didn't know what to do and then, just as my brain started to work again, I decided to turn back but Tyler's eyes caught me and it was too late.

"Mom? I have to go. I'll call you back later, okay?"

"Okay. We love you."

"Love you, too." I clicked off the phone and went on into the diner. I looked over at Tyler as he waved me over to his table.

"Hi." I said as I slid in across from him.

"What are you doing here?"

"I was just taking a walk. I live a few blocks away. Remember?"

"Oh. Right." He sounded like he had been a million miles away.

"What are you doing here?"

"Just had to get out. Be alone."

"Oh. I'm sorry. I can leave..." I said as I started up, but Tyler's hand quickly grabbed mine and he eased me back down.

"Please. I think I could actually use the company after all."

"What's the matter?"

"It's Dave. He was appointed the head of the Spectrum task force and when he asked me to help him, I thought I'd be able to talk some sense into him, but I don't know if I can support him in it anymore."

"You don't?"

"I just don't think Spectrum is a threat to anyone here. I think he's actually good."

"Me too." Tyler shot me a smile and my heart jumped.

"I told him that from the start. Dave is just so obsessed with hunting him down. To be honest, it's starting to affect our relationship. We never used to fight as much as we have been for the past few weeks."

"I'm sorry to hear that." I tried to disguise the hope in my voice. "Why did you come here?"

"I just had to get out and think. I usually come here for some private time," he said. I looked around. The diner was done in a classic fifties style motif but it was not as obnoxious as some others. The music was soft yet not so low you couldn't hear it and the whole place seemed rather quiet and calm.

"I've actually seen this place but have never been in."

"But you came in today." Tyler said with a wink.

"Are you implying that I planned this?"

"I'd never say such a thing." Tyler said with a smile.

We continued to talk and refreshingly, we managed to avoid the topics of boyfriends and old wounds. I told Tyler some horror stories of working at the cafe over a cheeseburger that came with a side of some of the best French fries I had ever tasted in my life. The waitress kept coming by and filling our coffee cups as we continued talking. The years that had been put between us seemed to have melted away and I realized I had forgotten what it was like to just sit with Tyler and talk.

Back in Blue Haven we would always find ourselves caught in such deep conversations. On several occasions we would sit down for a drink and before we knew what was happening, the day was gone and the establishment we were sitting in was closing.

We starting talking intensely about the food situation at the Blue Haven Community College when I looked outside and noticed the sun had gone down and the streetlights had come on. Tyler took notice as well.

"What time is it?" He asked as he checked his watch. "Do you realize we've been sitting here talking for four hours now?" He looked up at me.

"What? No way!"

"It's almost nine right now."

"Wow. I don't think we've talked this much in..." I said and my mind drifted to the past. To the easy, carefree days when our relationship had just begun. The lazy afternoons we would spend at the local park just staring up at the sky and talking about anything that would enter our minds.

"A long time." Tyler said, completing the thought.

"Yeah." I heard the front door of the diner open and suddenly a loud, boisterous voice shook me and Tyler from our reverie.

"Tyler!" Dave said. "There you are," he said as he slid in next to Tyler and wrapped his arm around him tightly. My heart stopped beating for a moment and it felt as though a fist of ice had reached into my chest and had my heart tight in its grip.

"Hey, Dave."

"Hi, Jason. What's going on here?"

"I was getting something to eat and Jason came by and I asked him to join me."

"Oh. Nice." Tyler didn't seem to pick up on the dubious tone of Dave's voice, but I did. His eyes found mine and I could see the fire burning inside. Part of me felt bad because I didn't want to intrude on their relationship, at least by principle, but another part of me was glad because clearly he saw me as a threat. That was promising.

"What brings you here?" Tyler asked as he kissed Dave gently.

"Just about finished with my shift. I was coasting by and I saw you in here and thought I'd see if we could squeeze in a little dinner together. It's been a while since we've done that, right?"

"That sounds nice, but I actually ate a little while ago. Sorry."

"Oh. That's fine." Dave said as he shot a look at me. "Did Tyler tell you about the promotion I got at work?"

"Yeah. You're the one in charge of the mob of villagers. Who's in charge of passing out pitch forks and torches?"

"I guess you agree with Tyler. You think this Spectrum nut is some kind of hero."

"So far as I can see that's how it's been looking."

"We don't know what he is. He could be an alien or something worse. He could be doing all these 'good deeds' just to suck us in so he can call in his freak buddies to kill us and take over this planet." Dave said. The conviction in his voice was sincere.

"Whatever he is, he's saving lives. If you ask me, it's those Drone Droids and trigger happy task forces that are kicking up the most dust."

"We do what we do for the safety of this city."

"And collateral damage is just an acceptable loss." Dave slammed his fist down on the table. His inner psycho was out for all to see. Every head in the diner turned to him and the moment just hung in the air.

"I think we should all take a breath and agree to disagree right now." Tyler said as he pulled Dave's arm back.

"Maybe I should go."

"Maybe you should." I looked over at Tyler and he could only offer a sympathetic look.

"I'll see you later, Tyler." I said as I got up and left the diner.

I got a few feet from the diner and looked around. I saw Tyler and Dave exchanging words and they didn't look like they were calm ones.

I was heading back home, but my thoughts kept skipping back to Tyler. Back at the diner, I thought what had happened could have been good, but the fact was that Tyler did not leave Dave to find me. He was still there trying to salvage what was left of their relationship. He wasn't giving up. I just wished he had been that committed to us.

I quickly ducked around a corner, released the suit and found the highest point in the immediate area. I felt too tired to really play super hero, but being Spectrum was the best and fastest way to banish the persistent memories of Tyler.

I reached the top of a nearby apartment building. It was several stories higher than my building and it afforded a perfect view of downtown. It just felt good to have the suit on. Soon, my thoughts began to calm and I was back in control.

"Impressive." A voice came from behind. I spun around and a familiar figure appeared before me out of the shadows.

"You. I know you. I saw you at the Neon processing plant."

"Good memory."

"You saw me there too, didn't you?"

"I did."

"Why didn't you say anything?"

"Because I appreciate the progress of potential."

"Potential?" The man walked along the edge of the building casually.

"Yes. Can I tell you a little secret? I'm the one who created Neon."

"Volt told me about you. Sur Reel, right?"

"Dear boy. Seems you just can't keep a secret these days. What Volt didn't tell you is what Neon really is."

"It's a drug. End of what I need to know."

"No. Actually Neon is a compound. Not a drug. It's a compound designed to create exceptional life. To be honest, I had to improvise the ingredients here. Most of what it takes to make Neon doesn't even exist here."

"Here? Are you telling me you're an alien?"

"Heavens, no. I'm a god."

"Excuse me?" I asked. He said the words so casually and easily, as though he were just mentioning his job in some form of polite conversation. He stopped and turned his back to me. He folded his arms behind his back and I saw his gnarled, rotted hands clasp each other and tighten as he stretched. A soft chuckle rumbled from his chest.

"You people here never cease to amaze me. You all think you have the whole universe figured out, but in reality, you couldn't be further from any kind of truth. I swear, sometimes I think your evolution has actually been going backward."

"Why are you here? What is this?"

"As I said, I'm a god. Or rather, a fallen god. I was sent to this planet as a punishment. I was charged with identifying and destroying a certain anomaly that could prove to be the beginning of the end of all creation," he said. I felt the question forming in my head, but before I could say it he put his finger up in order to silence me. "Before you even ask, yes. I believe you are that anomaly," he said and then turned to face me. His glare was hard and strong. A dark shadow under the rim of his top hat hid the top of his face from view, but I could see his eyes. Two milky gray orbs that somehow seemed to burn like fire. I put my arms down and began generating a charge in both my hands, ready to fire at a moment's notice. "However, I've been watching you. Studying you. Appreciating you."

"So, you're a fan?" I asked jokingly. He smiled slightly.

"I've found the one way you humans are so turned around and backward has been in the case of power. I know what true power is. I know what it takes to create life itself. I've seen the very gears of the universe at work so I, more than anyone, know the true nature of power."

"If you have a point, I'd love it if you could get there."

"Sorry. Sometimes I tend to go on. My point is that what I consider power, what I know to be power, is nothing to your race. Whereas, your people consider this..," he said and then suddenly he pulled out a fistful of dollars. "...To be power here. This! These inconsequential pieces of paper dipped in green ink. Those with this in abundance seem to hold dominion over the rest of you. They are given special privilege and consideration within your own government. For the past few decades, I have been working on this level, but then you came along. I could smell the stink of infinite power off you from the start. You have changed everything."

"How so?" Sur Reel then slid up closer to me and wrapped his bony fingers around my shoulders. The stench of his flesh was indescribable. It was like warmed up rotted flesh.

"Your power and my intellect and ambition. Put those together and there's nothing we couldn't accomplish. I've got the talent and you've got the vast, inexhaustible reserves of pure energy that I need to do what must be done."

"Really." I said as I shrugged his hands from me and turned away.

"Don't be like this. Don't act like you actually care for these things."

"Excuse me. I happen to be one of 'those things.'"

"No. You're not one of them. You never were. You're something more. You have been since the day you were born. This has been your destiny since you first drew breath. Your life has brought you to this place, at this moment for a reason."

He kept droning on about power and destiny but my eyes were glued downward. I could still see the diner a few blocks up the way and I watched as Dave and Tyler finally left it. It seemed whatever rift they were going through had subsided as they walked hand in hand to the parking lot in the back. I felt the blade dig deeper into my heart. The unbearable stench of Sur Reel filled my nostrils once more. "I know what you're feeling right now, and while I would love to be more sympathetic, I simply cannot be. These petty little games of the heart are so far beyond you."

"Look, I appreciate the courage it takes to expose this level of insanity, but I'm not interested in whatever you're selling."

"I'm offering you a chance to be the architect for the next phase in existence. With you, we could rewrite everything. You love that Tyler fellow? He can be yours. Everything you've ever wanted can be yours and I'm the only one who can make it happen for you. This is a partnership that was written in the stars. It has to happen," I turned to him. He was holding one of his disgusting looking hands out at me, waiting for me to take it. A god? I never imagined any kind of god looking like some kind of sideshow carnival barker crossed with a creepy pedophile. There was just something about his eyes. Something dark and predatory waited behind them, but with the discovery of the suit, my mind had broadened quite a bit. What if he were telling the truth? What if he could do what he claimed? I could have the life I have always dreamt of. The suit could finally do something good for me. I could use these powers to make Tyler mine once more and forever. It was tempting. All I had to do was say yes. I turned to Sur Reel, but before I could speak, a loud bang rang out from the diner's parking lot. I spun around and briefly I saw what looked like a couple of thugs disappear around the corner. I moved to leap off the roof, but Sur Reel grabbed me. "Don't waste your time. Come with me. You don't need them. You're not like them,"

"I'm not a murderer either." I said and pulled free of Sur Reel's grip. I leapt up off the roof and soared up the block to the Diner.

I landed on the roof and saw Tyler and Dave cornered by two gun toting thugs. Tyler was on the ground while Dave shielded him.

"We don't want any trouble." Dave said.

"Well, you got trouble, man." One of the thugs said.

"What do you want? Money? Here." Dave said as he pulled out his wallet and tossed it to them. The other thug kicked it away.

"No, man. We're on kind of a scavenger hunt. The last thing on our list is two dead cops. Just thought we could at least get one right now."

"Hold on, Ice." The other thug said as he pointed at Tyler. "I know that dude. He's a cop too!"

"Oh! You're kidding! Ain't that cute! The two piggies were about to make some bacon. Cool. We get two cops and two fags all in one hit." The first thug said as he lowered the gun to Dave's head. I could hear the gun being cocked, so I swung over and dropped down hard. I quickly swatted the gun away and kicked the thugs away. They fell back hard, but scrambled quickly to their feet.

"It's the freak, man!"

"I can friggin' see that, idiot!"

"Why don't you boys just move on?" I said. The gun toting thug was more focused on getting his gun back. He leapt forward and slid for it, but I snagged his hand as he grabbed the gun and with a quick squeeze, I felt his fingers break. He let out a blood curdling howl as he held his broken hand to his chest. His friend seemed to be a little slow and didn't seem sure what to do. He seemed to be hovering between running and trying to get the gun back. I took his moment of indecision and blasted him with a force beam, which drove him into a nearby wall. He fell to the ground in a heap. I turned around and saw Tyler and Dave huddled together. I walked over to them. "Are you all right?" I asked as my eyes fell upon Tyler. He looked a little scared, but no worse for wear.

"I'm fine, just got the wind knocked out of me." Dave quickly bolted up and pulled out his gun and trained it on me.

"You're under arrest!" He shouted. Tyler started to get up.

"Dave! He just saved our lives!"

"I have my orders. You are under arrest. Don't take another step."

"I just want to make sure..." I started, but suddenly Dave squeezed the trigger and fired at me. It took me by surprise, so I wasn't fast enough to block the bullet and I felt it tear through my leg. I screamed out in pain as the bullet seared through my flesh. I had never felt so much pain. I dropped to one knee and grabbed the injured leg tightly.

"Dave!" I looked up and saw Tyler pull the gun out of Dave's hands.

"He's wanted. It's my job to bring him in. When do you think I'm going to get another chance like this?"

"I get that, but come on! If he hadn't come along, we'd both be dead right now and you know it."

"I'm sorry, but I have a responsibility." Dave said.

"But not a gun." Tyler said as he dangled Dave's gun in front of him. Dave fumed for a moment.

"Fine. I won't shoot him, but I do have to arrest him." He growled. He then turned back to me and walked up and bent down to meet my eyes. "I don't give a shit what you did, freak. If Tyler weren't here, I would have put that bullet in your head. Count yourself lucky." He whispered. "Now. You have the right to remain silent..." He began, but as soon as the pain in my leg subsided, I threw my arm up and cracked him right in his nose causing Dave to fall back.

I stood up and a shock of pain shot through me like a bolt of lightning. It was like getting shot all over again. My vision blurred, but I could see Tyler running to Dave's side. I didn't have time to worry about the meaning of that. I had to get out of there. I felt a rush of power well up inside me and just like that, I was up in the air.

I flew back to the roof where I was speaking with Sur Reel, but he was long gone. I landed on the roof and sat down as quickly as I could. My leg hurt like a son of a bitch and I was still trying to catch my breath. I looked around and noticed a small slip of paper folded neatly along the edge of the rooftop. I got up and picked the paper up and opened it. There was just a short message scrawled across it.

'Hope it was worth it.'

I crumpled the note up and tossed it aside and crawled back to a small shady spot. I just needed a few minutes to catch my breath, along with my thoughts.

PART 3

17

Jason walked into the Lauvre Cafe for his afternoon shift with every hope he would be able to do so with little attention, but his pronounced limp was difficult to cover up. He was hoping the gun shot wound he suffered would have healed over, but the suit was only able to do so much.

"What happened to you?" Tristan asked as Jason walked by.

"I tripped. Fell down a few stairs in my building." Jason said. He pressed his hand onto his leg right over where he was shot. It still hurt, but not as much. It was a dull, aching pain but nothing he couldn't deal with.

"You think you'll be able to get through your shift?"

"Sure. I'm fine. It just looks worse than it really is." Jason said as he headed into the back.

He grabbed his apron and was tying it on when he looked out to the front and saw Tyler and Dave walking in together. Jason let out a frustrated sigh. Dave not only disliked Jason, but he also had a mad on for Spectrum as well. It didn't seem like there was any way to win, but despite that fact, he took a deep breath and walked out to take their order.

"Morning," Jason said. "What can I get for you two?"

"Just coffee. Black." Dave said.

"Same and a blueberry muffin." Jason jotted down the order and stepped away. He could hear Dave's husky voice whispering to Tyler about something. Jason couldn't make it out, but he had a pretty good idea what it was. Jason stepped behind the counter and started pouring two cups of coffee. Jason tried to block out all other noises so he could focus on what Tyler and Dave were discussing. Since the only other voices in the cafe were coming from the television, it wasn't hard. He couldn't make out exact words, but the tones were clear. Tyler sounded more passive while Dave's voice was growing with anger. A fight. Jason's heart beat a little faster. He knew it was wrong to be so happy about it, but he couldn't help himself.

As soon as he finished pouring the drinks, he spun around and snagged one of the fresh blueberry muffins from the display case and set it on a small, white plate. He put everything on a small tray and walked it over to the table. As he approached, Dave quickly quieted down.

"Here you go." Jason said as he set the order down. As he set the muffin before Tyler, he shot him a quick glance, which Tyler returned.

"Thanks." Tyler said.

"You're welcome,"

"Yes! Thank you." Dave said. Jason looked over at him and he could see Dave was not happy.

"Sure. Enjoy." Jason said and then hurried back to the counter to return the tray.

"Oh boy. He does not like you." Tristan whispered.

"I don't suppose he does."

"You know you're playing with fire there."

"What do you mean?"

"Coming between two people in a relationship is always a risky gamble."

"I'm not coming between them." Jason defended. Tristan merely smiled and let out a gentle laugh.

"Please. Every time Tyler comes in here, you can't do enough for him. Don't think that kind of customer service doesn't go unnoticed."

"I'm just good at my job."

"You're really going to deny this?"

"If you're implying I have some kind of plan to break them up, I don't."

"You don't have to tell me, but Dave over there seems to think different."

"He's just paranoid."

"Is he?" Jason shot him a cold stare.

"Yes."

"Okay. Fine. You have no designs on Tyler, but maybe on some subconscious level you flirt with him."

"Dave is only on edge because he caught me and Tyler together having a little dinner."

"Really?"

"We ran into each other. It wasn't planned, and Dave was on duty anyway. I was just keeping Tyler company."

"Look, Jay. I don't know the exact nature of your relationship with Tyler, but I know what I see. Whatever you claim to feel for him, the fact is you like him and it shows. Whether you want it to or not, it shows."

"Is there some kind of advice to go along with these insights?"

"I'm just telling you to be careful."

Tyler and Dave did not linger over their coffee for long and before Jason could have a chance to return to their table, they had already left leaving a meager tip behind. Jason cleared away the cups and the plate and went in the back to wash them, as he did every day.

As Jason dumped the cups into the soapy water in the sink, he heard his cell phone ring.

"Yes?" He asked.

"Just wanted to let you know the results have arrived." Heather said.

"This quickly?"

"I know some people. They made it happen."

"But, won't they say something?"

"Don't stress. No living being has seen these results. It was all done by computers. Besides, if anyone saw this stuff, they wouldn't have any idea what it was about."

"So what do the results say? What is this thing?"

"I'm not doing this over the phone. Come over to my place when you get off work and I'll walk you through it. It's very interesting."

"Are you kidding me? You're going to leave me hanging like this?"

"'Fraid so. See you later." Heather said and then clicked off.

The rest of the day seemed to drag on purpose. The minutes crawled by and all Jason could think of were the results of Heather's examination. His mind wandered and he dreamt of all the possible things the results could prove. Maybe the suit was alien in origin or perhaps it was some super secret government project that leaked out. Anything was possible after everything Jason had seen since being bonded to the suit. The universe seemed to be opening wider right in front of him.

The end of his shift finally arrived and Jason practically flew out the door and onto the street. He leapt onto his bike and powered through the mid-town traffic in record time.

As he swerved through the maze of cars and busses, he began to get a feeling of unease. It was as if there were eyes upon him. A sharp feeling of dread filled him and he slowed down to a stop and scanned the area quickly. It didn't seem there was anyone watching him, but he could still feel as though he were being studied. He sloughed it off and continued on his way.

Jason returned home and ran up to Heather's apartment, leaving his bike outside his own door. Before he could even knock, her door swung open.

"About time. Come in," she said. Jason walked in quickly and he started looking around in hopes of seeing the papers that had the answers he was looking for.

"Okay. Give it to me." Jason said excitedly. Heather plucked a large envelope off a nearby table and opened it up and pulled out a thick folder and opened it.

"Well," She began as she looked down at the pages she held. "It seems the suit naturally augments everything in your body. Strength, speed, everything. It also seems to be supercharging your immune system. As of this test, you have no viruses or bacteria in your body."

"That's irregular?"

"Yes. We always have something lurking in us. A dormant cold or allergy infection. You are one hundred percent clean."

"Wow. Cool."

"As for your powers, the suit acts like some kind of generator and battery. It generates all kinds of energy on several different wavelengths but it also stores energy as well."

"Well that's not really news to me."

"But I'm talking about any kind of energy or radiation. Whatever energy this thing encounters, it can create it and manipulate it. It must have tapped into your own personal magnetic field, which is how you have your magnetic powers. You probably can do some tricks with light as well."

"What about the electricity?"

"We have bio-electric energy inside of us as well."

"Okay. So I can do a lot great stuff. Fine. Great. Bottom line this for me. Is this thing alive? Is it an alien?" Heather looked at Jason with a troubled expression.

"It has a pulse."

"What?"

"The suit has a pulse. It is alive."

"Then it's alien?"

"That I don't know. It could be an ancient life form that has survived to this day or an artificial specimen cooked up in some lab."

"That doesn't really help me."

"You should also know it has a built in life support system."

"What?"

"When it's outside of your body, it breathes oxygen into your bloodstream. Also judging by its molecular structure, it seems to be super dense. It's about as strong as steel but as thin as silk."

"So a living suit of armor?"

"Essentially, yes. Bottom line here is whether it came from a test tube or someplace a thousand light years away, that suit is one powerful mutha."

18

When Jason had first learned that the suit he wore as Spectrum was actually a lifeform, he thought it was kind of creepy, but it didn't take long for him to adjust, but learning about the near limitless capabilities it possessed began to scare him. He had never been one who ever had access to such power before and as exciting as it seemed at first, once it crystallized in his mind and he started to see the reality of such power, he became unsure as to whether he should be responsible.

The growing media attention surrounding Spectrum didn't help either. It seemed every night there was some story or public diatribe either in favor of or against Spectrum. Unfortunately, there seemed to be more people on the 'against' side of the argument. Between Manicore's media machine and Police Chief Kelvin, the people of Towers City had been whipped into a state of near panic. They were being fed lies about Spectrum being an alien conqueror who only poses as a hero in order to study humans more closely with the ultimate goal of taking over the planet and seeding it with pods to create more of his kind. There were also some rumors flying around that said the suit was a new weapon of terrorism that our overseas enemies were testing.

Jason didn't seem to have anywhere to go anymore. With the

increased Drone Droid units patrolling the city, it wasn't safe to go out, but he could only take hearing the ignorant lies being spread about him for so long until he had to get out for some air.

He finally reached a crisis point and with little thought for his own well being, Jason switched into Spectrum and zipped out his skylight and headed toward no specific location.

It was a seemingly quiet night. He could see a few clusters of Drone Droids hovering around the downtown area, so he kept low and far from there.

He kept to the quieter neighborhoods. There wasn't usually much action to be had, but Spectrum hadn't come out for action. He just needed to clear his head.

He came upon a small, clustered neighborhood in the high rent district. It was a quaint spread with well polished, handsome homes and clean, freshly paved streets. Spectrum found a large tree that towered over one of the blocks and he found a place to perch. He looked out past the limbs and leaves of the tree and up to the sky. He stared at the star dotted canvas above and he let his mind drift into thought.

As his mind relaxed and began to really think for the first time in a long time, something suddenly dawned upon him. The dreams he was having when he first received the suit might not have been dreams after all, he thought. They had felt more than just dreams at first, and they might have been. It could have been the suit communicating with Jason. Telling him something about where the suit had come from. Then the scope of everything began to hit him. Alien worlds. Living weapons. How much more was out there? What had he gotten himself into? The responsibility of the suit was becoming much larger and all encompassing than Jason had previously thought.

Jason's thoughts were abruptly halted when he heard a loud, wooden crack from below. He sprang up and shot out of the tree. For days, Jason had the feeling that something had been stalking him. As though eyes he couldn't see were watching his every move.

Spectrum looked around quickly but saw nothing. A slight breeze blew by and the soft rustle of the leaves was all that filled the air.

Instead of resuming his seat, Jason moved on in hopes of leaving whoever, or whatever, was following him behind.

Jason got closer to the main hub of the city but was careful to keep as far from any Drone Droids as he could manage. He found that task to be easier than normal. The Drone Droid patrols were rather spread out and weren't very aggressive, which was different.

Jason found a perch to sit upon. He settled in and looked out over the city. The candy colored lights below glowed and flickered brightly and the faint noise of traffic could barely be heard from so high. Jason felt his worries leaving him.

His reverie was short lived, however, as he felt a warm blast erupt underneath him and before he knew it, he was being showered with debris and fire. He spun through the air and managed to get his bearings. He looked back to where the explosion originated and as the smoke settled, he saw some sort of horrific beast. It looked as though it was some kind of hybrid alien monster, human and machine. It was large and muscular with sickly looking skin and an inhuman, almost reptilian face. Its flesh had metal implants stuck inside of it along the arms and chest. It stared up at Jason with a set of piercing red, robotic eyes.

"Lab One engaging target." An electronic voice announced. The beast raised its arm and a large cannon popped out of its slimy flesh and fired two charges. Jason spun out of control as he dodged the onslaught. Jason swung around quickly and was about to fire off a charge of electricity, but as he did, he felt himself fall. Before he knew it, he was screeching down to the street like a bullet. He quickly refocused himself and halted his descent.

"Okay," he said to himself. "Can only do one thing at a time. Remember that."

Jason began climbing back up but as he did, he saw the creature coming down in a free fall. Before Jason could do anything, the creature snagged him as he fell past him and the both started falling to the streets below. Jason pulled himself free at last and the creature ended its journey down on its own.

There was an audible crunch as it hit the asphalt below. Jason floated down as a crowd began to form around the fallen form. Jason stood over the creature and looked upon it with a sincere curiosity. It was spread along the street in a small crater left by the impact. There was no blood. No brains or any signs that the creature was actually alive. Jason stooped down to get a closer look when the creature suddenly came back to life and lunged forward, tackling Jason down.

"Lab One. Online." The electronic voice said again. Jason took a breath and with one good push, knocked the creature away. Jason got to his feet quickly.

"So. Lab One's your name, huh?" The creature took an aggressive posture. As Lab One leapt forward, Jason shot up into the sky. He flew off toward somewhere he knew would be free of any other people.

Jason landed in the middle of Ophelia Park. It was the largest public park in Towers City and was named after the city founder's wife, Ophelia Towers. It was pitch black and quiet as a tomb, until the sound of Lab One's claws scratching against the ground was heard. Jason turned and Lab One landed a few feet away. "You're the thing that's been following me around! So. Where do you come from? Mars? Some planet I've never heard of?"

Lab One's only response was a forceful swipe at Jason. It leapt forward but Jason let out a bolt of energy and hit it in midair, which caused Lab One to fly back. It landed against the dirt hard and Jason could hear something break.

He ran over and saw some of the metallic components in Lab One's body had broken and he could see inside. There were gears and needles and lots of parts that looked more like surgical tools than parts for a robot. He leaned over to take a closer look when he heard a voice shout out.

"Halt!"

Jason turned to see a tall, strong looking woman wearing a futuristic looking black body suit standing before him. She had a bandana tied across her eyes with holes cut into it so she could see. It was difficult to see, but her eyes looked as though they were as black as Onyx. She had long, black hair that reached down to her legs and she held a large, thick sword in one of her hands. "You are known here as Jason Randwulf?"

"Here?"

"Yes. On Earth."

"Is there another choice? Where are you from?"

"I am hunter designate: Panther. First tier, class A hunter under order of the Xenosian Empire."

"Xenosian?"

"I am from Xenos," she said. "And you are under arrest for possession of stolen property. Surrender now, or perish."

19

Panther stood before Jason. Strong and fortified. Her stance was proud and fierce as she held her sword tightly in her hand.

"I am here to recover the stolen property. Release it now," she said.

"What stolen property? I've never stolen anything in my life! I sure as hell never stole anything from another planet."

"You bear the God's Blood."

"What? This?" Jason asked as he indicated to the suit.

"It was taken from my people many years ago. I have searched a long time for it."

"So that thing over there is your little bloodhound?"

"Lab One is a living, breathing bio-organism research center. It has been tracking you for quite some time now. Studying you. When the observation phase was completed, I was called in to re-capture the God's Blood."

"Why do you call this thing God's Blood?"

"Enough questions! Surrender it to me at once!" She barked.

"I can't."

"Then I shall take it by force." She then advanced on Jason quickly with her sword raised. He leapt back just as her blade came down and then lunged forward, tackling her to the ground. He thought he had her pinned pretty good, but she swung around underneath him and in a flash, she was free and was tossing Jason back like he was nothing.

As Jason got up, he saw Panther racing toward him and he threw out a shot of energy, but she effortlessly avoided it and then began hammering him with her bare hands. Jason did the best he could to deflect her attacks but she moved like a ninja on Speed.

"You're good." Jason said as he tried to catch his breath. Panther was in her attack pose, ready to go, without a drop of sweat on her forehead.

"I don't have orders to kill, but I will if I must."

"Okay. Let's calm down for a second. I'm sure we can work something out," Jason said. He looked past Panther and saw Lab One beginning to twitch and move. It began to reassemble itself and then it stood up. Panther turned as it began to stalk over toward them.

"Lab One. Stand down. Your mission is complete."

"Lab One. Online." It said as it got closer. Panther turned to Lab One and seemed to attempt to stop it, but it easily pushed her aside as it continued forward. It came up on Jason and then he took a step back, but with little effort, Lab One grabbed Jason, crouched down and leapt up like a rocket sending it and Jason up into the air and back toward the city.

Jason and Lab One shot across the sky and they landed in an explosion of dust and smoke in the middle of what was once a quiet, well maintained block of trendy stores in the arts district of Towers City.

As the dust settled, Jason could see Lab One charging forward like a rabid beast. It lunged at Jason and slashed and bit with lightning speed. Jason pushed back with a blast of energy and knocked Lab One into a nearby parked car. Jason stepped back and watched as Lab One quickly recovered from the impact and crawled away from the car which then had a Lab One sized dent that crumpled the entire body of the car. Jason watched Lab One carefully and while he wasn't very familiar with the creature, even he could tell something was wrong. The wires were crossed and whatever it was programmed to do had been scrambled. It was a machine out of control, plain and simple.

Lab One quickly rallied its strength and went back after Jason, but instead of attacking like an animal, it shifted and attacked like a human. It grabbed Jason by the neck and sent him flying high into the sky with one well placed punch. Jason crashed into the fourth floor of a nearby apartment building and soon lights began to come on and people started to take notice of the brawl transpiring right in their backyards. Jason tried to get up and get back to the fight, but before he could get up, Lab One leapt up on top of him and started pounding on him with everything it had. The suit cushioned most of the impact, but it still hurt and as Jason was pinned down, enduring the barrage, his mind seemed to break for a split second. He thought of all the people and things that have been coming after him since he received the suit. The freaks seeking power. The curious who only want to study him. The whole world beating a path to his door for their own ends when all he wanted to do was make the world better and for all the good he did do, the one thing he wanted most in the world still eluded him. The one person not interested. Tyler. Tyler who was back with David. Still with David.

Jason felt his anger rising and something in him was feeding it and making it grow. He suddenly popped back and with a single thought, he managed to create a shock powerful enough to knock Lab One off of him. Jason got up quickly and shot down to the street like a bullet and he landed just as Lab One was getting up again. Jason charged forward, but Lab One grabbed him by his head and flung him down the street into a grouping of cars, which caused a massive explosion that created a huge fireball. Lab One stood proudly as it watched the flames disappear into the night sky. Panther arrived on the scene moments later to find Lab One gloating over its victory.

"No!" She barked as she came upon Lab One. "You were under strict orders! You destroyed the subject. You will be brought to the council for disciplinary charges," Lab One just sneered at her, grabbed her and tossed her aside like she was nothing. Panther quickly pulled out her sword and prepared for Lab One's next attack, but it was too little too late as Lab One barreled down on Panther and crushed her into the side of a building. She looked up at Lab One and she could see better than anyone could, it had somehow reached sentience. It was under its own power and clearly the freedom was too much. It didn't know what to do so it was falling back to its most primal, basic programming. It stood over her with its claws shining and its eyes alive with the lust for blood. She tried to move, but her arms were weak and she felt she was still in shock. She tried to grip her sword, but her fist couldn't tighten enough around the hilt.

"Hold it!" A voice called out. Lab One looked over its shoulder and past the fire and cracked asphalt. Through the smoke and excited murmurs of onlookers, it saw Spectrum standing at the end of the street. Stalwart and steadfast. Power trickling off his body. Lab One turned to him with particular interest. Jason felt all the energy he could muster fill his body. He looked down and his arms were shaking. There was a buzzing in his head and his vision was becoming blurred. By instinct, he launched himself forward and he streaked toward Lab One, who was also stampeding toward his prey. They met in the middle with an enormous release of pure energy. The force of their impact broke every piece of glass for two blocks and caused the street and sidewalks to crack and break. When the dust settled, Spectrum stood over the broken Lab One, still buzzing with power.

"You destroyed it." Panther said. Jason looked up and saw Panther standing before him holding her arm. Blood traced down her cheeks and she walked with a significant limp. Jason quickly ran over to her.

"I think we should talk away from the audience."

Jason took Panther back to the park, leaving the very confused and frightened cluster of onlookers even more confused and frightened.

As Jason helped Panther find a bench to sit on, she looked up at him in amazement.

"You okay?" He asked.

"I'm sorry?"

"Are you injured? You feel good?"

"My wounds will heal. You destroyed Lab One."

"I'm sorry. It just looked like he was going to kill you and he really kind of pissed me off."

"You saved my life."

"Hasn't anyone ever done that before?" Jason asked as he sat down with Panther.

"I have not needed another's help in that respect before."

"Really? I would have thought for an alien bounty hunter, having your life saved would be kind of an almost every day thing."

"You are a most unusual being."

"Thanks. So, what is all this about you taking the God's Blood?"

"The God's Blood, your suit, is a life form born from an ancient crystal on my home world. A long time ago, Xenos was in a period of civil war. When the God's Blood was discovered, it was used to arm the many factions in the war. It was a dark time in our history. After the fight was over, the council chose to save the last bit of the God's Blood and bequeath it to a chosen warrior so that our people will never forget the struggle that earned us our freedom and that the God's Blood may be used to preserve life instead of taking it, as it was used all too often to do. Years ago, before the God's Blood could be passed on, it was stolen from us."

"And somehow wound up here. On me."

"It's been the mission of the entire Hunter Academy to retrieve the God's Blood from where ever it had been taken."

"Well, I'd love to give it to you, but I really don't know how I can. I mean, I got outfitted with this thing kind of by accident myself. And I think if I take it off, I might die. It's pretty attached."

"Then I have failed."

"I'm sorry. But if it makes you feel any better, I'm using it to do good."

"I can see that now, yes. But for the God's Blood to go to an off worlder." Panther said with a deep, sorrowful tone. Jason thought for a moment.

"So what now?"

"I must go back to my home and report my failure. I will accept whatever punishment they see fit to give me."

"But what about me? I mean, you know where I am. Won't they just send another hunter for me?"

"Perhaps, but as you have saved my life, I owe you a life debt as well. In honor of this, I will report that the God's Blood was destroyed."

"What? You will?"

"Yes. No further expeditions will be made here. You will be safe."

"Thanks. I'm sorry for you though. I wish I could help you more."

"You have done all anyone could do. I thank you and I shall wish you peace for all your days. Farewell, Spectrum," she said as she stood up. She pulled out a small device from a pocket in her suit and with a single button, a small door of light appeared in the air. She walked on through into the light and as soon as she did, it closed and all was as it was. The night was eerily quiet and Jason was ready to go home.

20

The morning sun rose over Towers City and it felt as though all the madness of the previous evening was washed away and everything reset back to normal.

Jason was buried under his sheets, fast asleep. His alarm clock began to blare, but with one well placed fist, he silenced it with little regard to what he may have been late for. All he wanted was to sleep and recharge.

The perfect silence was broken as a manic pounding came from his door.

"Good morning!" Heather sang from the hallway outside.

"Sleeping!" Jason barked from his bed. The pounding continued. "Sleeping!" Jason shrieked once more and then it seemed Heather gave up. Seconds later, the sound of a key being inserted into a lock was heard and the door swung open.

"You should know by now, I don't scare easy," she said as she walked in.

"Please. I'm begging. Give me one more hour before you say another word. Just one more hour." Jason pleaded. Suddenly, Jason felt Heather's weight rest at the foot of his bed. He peered out of his shelter of blankets and saw Heather sitting across from him holding the morning paper in her hand. She was holding it up in a way that displayed the front page rather prominently. It took him a few seconds for his eyes to focus, but once they did he could see the picture splashed across the front page had been taken the night before after he had fought off Lab One. Jason bolted forward and snagged the paper.

"You finally made the front page." Heather said.

"Who took this picture?"

"Never mind that. What made you think you could pull a stunt like that and not tell me all about it the minute you got back?"

"I really didn't understand what was going on myself. Some monster attacked me out of the blue and then I was talking to this woman with long hair. She told me about the suit..."

"Whoa! Hold on. She knew about the suit?" Heather asked. Jason hadn't intended to say anything. All the strangeness in his life was bad enough without letting aliens into the mix.

"She apparently knew what it was and where it came from."

"Well? Where does it come from?"

"I really don't want to talk about this right now. Last night was just a really weird night and I want nothing more than to lie here and forget every bit of it."

"Fine. I won't press." Heather said as she took the paper back. "But I must say. Bravo on all the collateral damage. I mean, when you and that suit party, you party."

"I wasn't trying to do all that."

"I know."

"It was mostly that creature. Anything about it in the article?"

"Just that it got cleaned up along with everything else courtesy of Manicore Industries."

"What?"

"Yeah. Manicore was first on site to mop up the mess you left behind. They're also footing the bill for the street and building repairs."

"Very generous of them."

"Just their way of buying another piece of the city."

"Anything about me?"

"Not a whisper, but then it seems whoever reported this story arrived after you had left the party, but anyone who's been paying attention knows this catastrophe has Spectrum written all over it."

"Thanks. Get out." Jason said as he tossed one of his pillows at Heather and with a wink and a smile, Heather breezed back out and left Jason to his rest.

Stoyan Amazu was at his desk going over the morning reports, as usual. He was Augustus Manicore's most trusted employee. He knew all the secrets and was the second most powerful person under the Manicore umbrella.

He adjusted the glasses that rested across the slender bridge of his nose as he started looking up the daily sales reports just as his phone rang. He pushed the speakerphone button without so much as a flinch.

"What?"

"Mr. Amazu? A reporter is calling..."

"Give him the official statement that was released earlier this morning."

"But..."

"I'm very busy right now. I don't have time to field stupid questions that I've already answered. Isn't it your job to absorb these annoyances, Ms. Thorpe?"

"I suppose it is, sir, yes."

"Then do your job or pack your things. Understood?"

"Yes, sir. Sorry, sir."

Stoyan clicked off the phone and went back to his work. He had been fielding questions from the press since four in the morning concerning the disturbance of the previous night. It seemed the eyewitness accounts weren't good enough, and there was also a lot of speculation about the mysterious creature that was found on site. Some were concerned that it was an alien or some rogue government experiment that had gotten loose.

The press release that had been written explained away most of everything and left enough room for expansion on some explanations, should the need arise. Stoyan's phone buzzed again and he pushed the button ready to snap at his assistant again, but before he could open his mouth, another voice came over the speaker.

"Stoyan." The cold, hollow voice said.

"Mr. Manicore." Stoyan said as he sat up to attention.

"Any news on the subject?"

"Not yet, sir, but I'm sure R & D will be done soon."

"Put a fire under 'em! I realize tinkering around with that thing can be rather tempting for them, but I need to know what it is and where it came from. And what else it can do."

"I will check on them right now."

"See that you do." Manicore said and then clicked off.

Stoyan went down to the Research And Development department and saw the entire staff hard at work dissecting the creature. It looked as though there were several teams splitting the various chores the task entailed. As Stoyan stepped off the elevator, a tall, bespectacled doctor in a clean, white lab coat greeted him.

"Mr. Amazu."

"Dr. LaMont. How goes the project?"

"It's all rather fascinating really. I had some med teams in place to study the creature's physiology, but when we opened it up, we found very little organic material."

"What?"

"It looks like a living creature, for the most part, but inside it's more like a robot. Come with me." Dr. LaMont said as he led Stoyan further into the room. It seemed every last bit of the creature had been taken apart and was being inspected with meticulous care. They came upon the largest work area and Dr. LaMont unveiled the creature to Stoyan. It was laid out on a large operating table with its chest wide open. "It's difficult to tell what this thing was made for or for what purpose, but as far as I can see it was used as some kind of research tool."

"Excuse me?"

"We found medical equipment inside of it as well as storage devices for biological samples."

"This thing was a research lab? A walking talking research lab?"

"That's the way it's shaping up, yes."

"Then I guess my next question would be what exactly was it studying?" Dr. LaMont looked back at him and carefully removed his glasses and then smiled.

"That, I think, you are going to be very happy about."

21

Jason arrived at the cafe and for the first time since he began working there, he was glad to be there. It felt normal and he felt grounded as he walked in. He was comforted to see what he expected to see. There was Tristan behind the counter on the phone with his sister, trying to resist the urge to tear his hair out as they talked.

Jason breezed by with an effortless wave as he went on into the kitchen and reemerged in his apron, ready for whatever the day held for him.

"You're late." Tristan said as he hung up the phone.

"I overslept. I'm sorry." Jason said.

"I would give you shit for it, but honestly, there hasn't been a single damn customer in here all day, so I guess it really doesn't matter. Maybe we should switch to an on-call schedule system."

"Don't. Please. This place isn't much, but it's better than nothing." Jason begged as he began his daily duties.

The day went on with few surprises. A few regulars came in for their usual cup of coffee and pastry. The floors were swept at least three times an hour and Jason and Tristan wound up spending most of their time watching television.

It was about fifteen minutes until the end of Jason's shift when

Tyler walked in dressed in full uniform. He nodded to Jason and Tristan as he took a seat. Jason walked over with a nervous smile.

"Hey." Jason said as he handed him a menu.

"Hi."

"Why don't you ever sit at the counter?"

"What?"

"It's nothing big, but it just kind of makes me curious. Everyone who comes in here usually goes for the counter, but you always sit at one of the tables. Why?"

"I don't know. I guess that's just what I'm used to. Why are you asking me now?"

"I guess I just really noticed. So, do you really need that menu or do you already know what you're having?"

"I'm not sure. I'm not even very hungry."

"Then why are you here?"

"I guess I wanted to talk to you," Jason's heart leapt up a bit. They hadn't spoken since the diner and that had been the most personal conversation they had ever had since Jason got to Towers.

"Really." Jason said, trying to sound cool.

"Yes. You remember that talk we had back at that diner?"

"Uh, I think so. Yeah."

"It was nice, wasn't it? I mean, I can't remember the last time we had a chance to talk like that."

"It's been a long time. It was a good talk though. Brought back a lot of good memories."

"Yeah. I've been thinking a lot since then. About things."

"You have?" Jason's heart was racing. It was happening just as he had imagined it so many times before. This was how Tyler was going to tell him he was finally leaving Dave because he still loved him. Jason closed his eyes and the feeling of the universe finally opening up and letting in the goodness overcame him.

"Yes. Dave was real upset about it. We worked it out, don't worry." Tyler said. Jason's heart sank to the floor. "It's just I'm not sure if I can really see you anymore. I don't think Dave's comfortable with it."

"Excuse me? Dave doesn't like me so that means we can't see each other? I know we have a deep history, but we're still friends too. Aren't we?"

"You know we are, Jay, but I love Dave and I know how he gets. Maybe if we just kind of stay out of each others' orbits for a while, he'll mellow out and we'll be cool again. Until then..."

"Oh. So, this is good bye."

"Just for now. I'm sorry it has to be like this, but I have to think of my future."

"With Dave."

"Yes," Tyler said. Jason took a deep breath and while he knew the pain was obvious, he did his best to pretend he was doing a good job of hiding it.

"Fine. If that's how you feel."

"It is. Again, I'm really sorry."

"Sure."

Tyler smiled quickly, got up from his seat and hurried out the door into the flow of foot traffic. Jason retreated back to the counter and put his head down on it.

"Sorry. That was scathing." Tristan said as he gently stroked Jason's hair.

"Am I still alive? I could have sworn I felt my heart pop."

"No. You're still alive."

"Damn."

Jason chose to walk his bike home after his shift. He wasn't in the mood to deal with afternoon traffic. As he walked, all he could hear were Tyler's words ringing in his head. 'I love Dave' kept echoing in his ears. He could see the letters of the words and the more he thought about it, the angrier he became. As he turned the corner to his home, his phone rang.

"Yes?"

"Jason? Don't come home!" Heather said urgently.

"What? Heather?"

"Just don't come home! It's not safe!"

"What do you mean? Heather, what's going on?"

"I can't talk now. Just stay away!" she said and then clicked off. Jason's curiosity was bubbling. He was just a block away from home and he just couldn't resist to see what was going on. He hurried to the corner, turned around and saw a swarm of police cars parked in front of his building. His heart nearly stopped. He quickly fumbled for his phone and dialed Heather again. It rang a few times and then a man's voice came on.

"Who is this? Who's calling this number?" The voice said. Jason quickly hung up. He looked up and saw Heather being escorted out of the building by two cops. Her hands were in cuffs and they put her in one of the police cars as though she were a criminal. Jason turned back and just headed in the opposite direction. He wasn't sure where he was going to go. He was more confused about why the police were arresting Heather and what they were doing at the apartment house in the first place. He looked down at his phone and thought to himself how badly timed Tyler's idea to stay away from each other was. He quickly pushed the speed dial and heard the ring tone hum over the line.

"Hello?" Tyler asked

"Tyler. I know we talked about our situation earlier, but I'm kind of freaking out right now."

"Jason? What's going on?"

"I don't know. I was headed home and when I got there, the police were everywhere. They arrested Heather."

"Why?"

"Does the tone in my voice make you think I know why this is happening?"

"Okay. Sorry. I'm at the station. I'll ask around and see what's going on. I'll call you later. Okay?"

"Okay. Thanks." Jason said and clicked off his phone.

Hours went by and there was no word from Tyler. Jason thought of going back home, but he wasn't sure what would be waiting for him there. As the sun came down, Jason switched into the suit and found a peaceful perch on a nearby apartment house a few blocks from his. It was a good vantage point. From there he could see that the police were still hovering around his building. It had lightened a bit, but there were still a couple cruisers and every once in a while a police copter would fly by. Jason's patience was wearing thin and he came to the conclusion that answers weren't going to come to him. He had to find them. He took off into the sky and headed toward downtown. He wasn't sure what he was going to be looking for but at the very least he might be able to break Heather out of jail.

When Jason arrived to the heart of the downtown district, the first thing he noticed was that the entire city seemed to be on high alert. There were more police patrols and more Drone Droids swarming around than he had ever seen. Something had the city in a state of panic, but he had no idea what it could have been. Suddenly, his phone began to ring. He found a quiet alley to land in and he quickly answered.

"Yes?"

"Jason?" Heather asked.

"Heather! What the hell is going on?"

"They know."

"What? Who knows what?"

"They know who you are. Manicore dissected that monster thing and they found DNA information on you. They know you're Spectrum." Heather said. Jason felt his legs go numb for a moment.

"So all these cops are out looking for me?"

"Yes."

"Why did they get you?"

"Manicore is charging me with trespassing. They found surveillance footage of us in their lab. They also fired my father."

"I'm sorry."

"It's not your fault. Don't worry about me. I'll be able to make bail no problem. You need to get the hell out of town. Now."

"I can't."

"Yes, you can. Get out of here and never use that suit again. Just disappear."

"I'm not going to run."

"Look, you've got some power, but you can't fight every policeman in the city, much less those Drone things they've got now. And it won't be long until the military gets involved. It's suicide."

"If I run now, I'll be running forever."

"The only alternative is to just turn yourself in."

"If that's what I have to do, then I'll do it."

"Jason! No! You'll just end up on an operating table, getting cut into bite sized pieces."

"The cops won't do that."

"Who's talking about the cops? Manicore's going to make you disappear long before the cops can get a hold of you."

"I'm going to fix this. Just sit tight. Okay?"

"Don't do anything stupid."

"I'll see you soon."

Jason returned to his apartment building and much to his relief, it seemed the police had abandoned their stakeout at last. The cop cars were gone and everything looked to be quiet and normal. Jason landed on the street and ran inside. Jason hurried to his unit and pushed open his door. His entire apartment had been ransacked. They had gone through everything. It seemed that they thought the suit was something Jason could take on and off and were hoping to find it there, or that's what Jason assumed. He looked around at the chaos around him and despite himself, he felt tears stream out his eyes.

He sat down and a feeling of total powerlessness wash over him. He didn't know what to do. There was no bad guy to beat up. There was no victim to rescue. He was being hunted like an animal and Heather was right. It was only a matter of time before they caught up with him. Jason took a deep breath and stood up determined to make a plan as he retracted the suit. He ran to his closet and changed his clothes quickly. He pulled on the biggest, most baggy clothes he had and topped it off with a hat to hide his face. He checked himself in the mirror quickly and was pleased. He didn't look good, but he didn't look identifiable either. Jason turned to the door and as he did, there was a knock at it. Jason walked over slowly and checked the peephole. Tyler was standing on the other side. He quickly opened it up.

"Tyler," Jason said.

"Jason," Tyler's tone was odd and stiff.

"You heard."

"Are you kidding? That's all anyone's talking about now."

"What are you doing here?"

"We got word you were here. You should have known the building was still under surveillance."

"Damn." Jason said to himself.

"Look, I convinced Dave to let me come in first. I was hoping I could help you surrender. Peacefully. I don't want you to get hurt."

"That's big of you."

"I'm serious. You know I've always thought Spectrum was doing good. I hate it that it's coming out like this. I think you could have been something really special. I think you still could be, but you have to play ball. You could come out of this thing alive."

"Not likely. Once they get their claws on me, I'm going to get cut and diced like a frog in a biology class."

"Dave promised me...."

"Screw Dave and his promises. Since it's looking like these are the last few hours of my life, I feel I should say this. Dave is a selfish, obnoxious jerk who doesn't respect you and would sell you down the river if it meant he could be Kelvin's lap dog."

"Wow. How long have you been holding onto that?"

"A long time. I'm sorry but that's how I see it."

"Well, then I guess you just see what you want to see, but despite your bitterness, I still care about you. Come with me now, and I promise you won't be hurt," Tyler said. Jason thought for a moment.

Him versus the entire city. His powers against an army with guns and tanks and all sorts of artillery. It would be a long fight, and Jason could not see him winning it. He turned to Tyler and was about to take his hand when suddenly light flooded the room from outside. Jason spun around and troopers came crashing through the windows and they trained their guns on him. The sound of a helicopter roared over the madness. More troops filed in from below. Jason turned back to Tyler, who was shaking his head and offering a sad, sympathetic expression. Jason bolted back to a set of stairs that led up to the roof. He dashed up and burst through the door at the top, but as he reached the roof, he found himself surrounded by a platoon of Towers City Police choppers.

"Freeze!" A voice from one of the choppers blared. "You are under arrest. Do not move or we will open fire. Lethal force has been authorized."

Jason stepped back as the copters closed in. The laser sights from the rifles the troops inside were packing danced through the night sky all around him.

"I'm sorry," Jason turned and saw Tyler walking toward him, and just past him, Jason saw Dave storm out. He was holding a rather large gun and had both hands gripped around the trigger. Jason let the suit out quickly and he went right into defense mode.

"Good work, Zane. You flushed him out like a pro." Dave said.

"You said you would give me an hour to get him to surrender."

"Sorry, babe, but I never was very patient, but don't worry. He's a big boy. He knows what's going down here. If he plays nice, he might live to see the sun come up tomorrow. You do understand that, don't you, Jay?"

"Yes." Jason growled. "I understand everything perfectly." Jason then spun around and let out a bolt of energy and hit one of the copters, knocking its rotors out of commission and sending it crashing to the street below.

"Jason! No!" Tyler shouted.

"That's it. You're going down." Dave said sharply as he lined his shot. Tyler ran out in front of Spectrum in hopes of blocking Dave's bullet, but he squeezed the trigger too quickly. Jason quickly grabbed Tyler, shoved him aside and deflected Dave's shot, which went up and struck one of the other copters' gas line, which caused it to burst into flame and spin out of control. Jason hurried to Tyler.

"Are you okay?"

"I'm fine. Thanks," Jason looked at Tyler and something over came him. The mask split open and without a thought Jason pressed his lips to Tyler's. Suddenly, an enraged Dave pulled Jason from Tyler.

"Son of a bitch!" He roared as he rammed his fist against Jason's face. "I knew all along, you know. I knew what you were thinking. From the first day I knew you still loved him. I knew you wanted him, but he's mine now. He's mine, and you're dead." Dave said and continued to beat Jason.

"Dave! Stop it!" Tyler barked as he pulled Dave away. As Dave's rage crested, he threw out his arm and clipped Tyler across his chin, which threw him down to the ground. Upon seeing this, Jason quickly sorted himself and stood up to his full height just as Dave turned back to him.

"Don't you ever touch him like that again." Jason growled. Dave threw his fist in a punch, but Jason caught it easily and with little effort, he squeezed and could feel the bones in Dave's hand cracking easily under his pressure. Dave pulled back quickly and started firing his gun at Jason, and as he did, each shot was deflected easily. When Dave's gun was empty, he bolted for Jason and tried to tackle him down, but Jason threw him aside easily. Suddenly a spotlight came down upon them all and the largest of the police copters descended upon the roof.

"Fire!" Dave called out and suddenly a storm of bullets rained down upon them.

"Dave! No!" Jason tried to generate a protective shield large enough to cover the roof, but just as he did, Tyler was hit several times by stray bullets.

"Tyler!" Tyler's lifeless body fell into a heap at his feet and for Jason, everything stopped. He looked over to Dave who seemed to be in a state of shock. Jason then looked up at the helicopter above and then he felt nothing but rage. Jason blew up in a spectacle of blue sparks and began firing out beams of electric energy left and right, blasting every helicopter or Drone Droid within range. He moved with ease and simplicity. It was as though his arms were reaching up and tearing apart everything he could reach.

Before long, the sky was empty and smoke was billowing up from the wreckage of the felled copters below. Jason then turned his attention to Dave who was bent down at Tyler's body. In one fluid movement, he pushed Dave away and knelt down by Tyler. He placed his hand on Tyler's cheek. He was already getting cold. Jason slid his hand under Tyler's head and tilted his head so their eyes met.

"I'm sorry," Jason said. Tyler smiled slightly. He opened his mouth, but nothing came out except a small trace of blood that slid along the ridge of his jaw. He then shook his head slowly and as quickly as that, the light and warmth in his eyes faded away. Sobs began to rip through Jason as he placed his head down on Tyler's still chest.

"You killed him."

"What?" Jason asked as he turned his head around.

"This is all your fault. You killed Tyler." David said with more strength. Jason stood up and turned to Dave.

"You have the balls to stand there and tell me that I caused all this?"

"None of this would be happening if it weren't for you. If you had turned yourself in from the start it wouldn't have come to this! You killed Tyler!"

Something snapped in Jason's mind and although he wasn't aware of his movements, he lunged forward at Dave and tackled him down.

"You're the one who gave the order to fire! His blood is on your hands! You killed him, Dave! You killed the only man I ever loved!"

Jason shouted. His hands quickly morphed into long claws and with every bit of anger he could muster, he stabbed them into Dave's chest. He dug in deep and felt his blood seep up. He could feel Dave's beating heart become still as he saw the life fade from Dave's eyes. "Now you can rot in hell." Jason stood up and looked down at Dave's lifeless body but felt very little relief or satisfaction. Tyler was gone and nothing could bring him back.

"Base. We have two men down. Repeat, two men down. Please advise." A meek voice said from behind. Jason turned and saw a few men from Dave's command standing before him.

"Take down the target. Lethal force is authorized." The voice over the radio said. Jason then realized he had just murdered a police officer and it was likely he'd be blamed for Tyler's death as well. Jason quickly leapt up to the air and took off like a shot into the night.

"Base. Target has fled the scene."

"Putting out an APB. All units be on the look out for Jason Randwulf, AKA Spectrum. Shoot on sight. Those are your orders."

22

Jason kept to the shadows as the police swarmed through the city. It felt as though Hell had broken out all over Towers City. Every street had patrols going up and down in search of Spectrum and the air was crackling with radio messages going between the various units. They were out for blood, which wasn't surprising. Two officers down was not a small thing.

Jason had been flying around all over the city in search of one place he could stop and catch his breath, but it seemed the entire city was under lock down. He couldn't even change out of the suit and disappear into a crowd since the police had his real identity as well as his alter ego. There was no place to run to and no place he could hide. At least, not for long.

He was huddled in a small alley off a small street. It seemed safe enough. It was dark and there weren't many people around. In fact, the only person Jason could see was some old cab driver sleeping through his shift in his car. He had the radio on and Jason could hear it. A news report came on and Jason's ears pricked up quickly.

"Police are now fully mobilized throughout Towers City in search of the individual known as Spectrum, who has now been identified as Jason Randwulf. If you have any information as to the whereabouts of the fugitive, you are advised to call the Towers City police right away. He is wanted currently not only for public endangerment, but now murder as well. The suspect was seen killing two armed Towers City police officers. Officer Tyler Zane and David Fordham were killed in the line of duty as they tried to apprehend Spectrum. A million dollar reward is available to any information leading to the arrest, capture, or death of Jason Randwulf." The reporter went on to say. Jason took a step and nudged against a nearby trash can, causing it to fall over. The cab driver roused and looked over in Jason's direction. The look of recognition was clear.

"Hey!" The cab driver called out. "Police! He's over here! Spectrum!" He continued to yell. Lights began to shine down from above and the garbled static of radio transmissions filled the air. Jason quickly bolted up into the sky and he heard the sound of what seemed like a thousand guns going off after him. A few bullets whizzed past him but soon he was too high up for them to follow.

Jason finally found a place he could settle for a bit. The Towers City National Cemetery. Jason went deep into the memorial park and found the oldest part of it. That was where all the trees were, and they were large and overgrown. A perfect place to hold up until morning. Once the sun came up he would have a plan, or so he hoped.

Jason found the darkest, most overgrown spot he could and settled behind the largest gravestone he could find. As he huddled against the marble statue of an angel looking up to Heaven, the whole day caught up with him. Tyler was dead. He was dead and worse, they were saying that he killed him. He couldn't stand losing the love of his life, but being blamed for his death was almost too much for him to bear.

"Well, well, well." A sinister voice called. Jason leapt to his feet and looked around. He saw Sur Reel laying across a couple of gravestones and looking at him with some kind of playful smile. "It seems we've gotten ourselves into quite a bit of trouble, now haven't we?"

"Go away." Jason barked. Sur Reel jumped up from his perch and danced over to Jason.

"Now. Don't be like that. I know what it's like to have a bad day," he said as he reached out to gently stroke Jason's cheek, but Jason slapped his hand away. "It seems rather rude for you to be so short when all I'm trying to do is make you feel better."

"So. How long have I got?"

"I'm sorry?"

"You've no doubt called the cops. How long before the entire police brigade lands on top of my head?"

"I have no intention of alerting the police."

"Then why are you here? To gloat? Are you here just to taunt me? The only man I've ever loved is dead and I killed a man. I don't give a shit about what you have to say to any of that."

"My friend. You totally misunderstand. I have not come to add to your burden. I have come to ease it. You remember what we talked about before?"

"About you and me teaming up?"

"Yes! That offer is still on the table, and frankly, I can't imagine you saying no now. You really have nothing left here, do you?"

"I guess not."

"So say yes. Join me. You don't owe those people anything anymore. You know the real reason they're after you now? They fear you. They're jealous of you. They want to take from you what makes you special only because they have nothing of their own. If it can't be them, it can't be you. There is another world where you can be who you were really meant to be."

"I guess I really don't have anything holding me here, do I? Fine."

"Excuse me?" Sur Reel asked with some bit of surprise.

"I'll do it. You and me."

"Well, that's fine. Wonderful." Sur Reel said as he approached Jason.

"So, how does this work?"

"Well, just close your eyes and leave the rest to me," Sur Reel said as he pulled out a small device from his back pocket. With a quick flick of the wrist, a sharp dagger popped out and he placed his hand on Jason's back. "There is just one thing I should tell you first."

"What?" Sur Reel then raised the dagger up and quickly stabbed it into Jason's back.

"You only get one chance to come willingly with Sur Reel. You see, I don't ask nicely the second time. I really only offered to include you as a nicety. I really don't need you. Just your power, which I'm currently draining from that marvelous suit of yours." He hissed as Jason felt the power in his body surging through him and bleeding out just as quickly. He felt the sharp, piercing blade cutting through his flesh, past the suit. The surging stopped abruptly and Jason fell to the ground. His arms were weak and his vision was going fuzzy. He looked up and saw Sur Reel standing over him tauntingly.

"So, now I leave you this world and the mess you've made of it. The police should be here soon, though, so you won't have to suffer for much longer." Sur Reel said as he turned away. He held up his dagger and stabbed it into the air, but much to Jason's amazement, it caught something. A spark of light lit up and as Sur Reel dragged the dagger down, the light grew brighter and soon a hole of light had formed and Sur Reel walked into it and disappeared. Jason struggled to his feet. He looked over and saw the police approaching and then back to the hole. With little deliberation, he lunged forward and dove into the light before it disappeared.

23

Jason awoke after what seemed like years of sleep. He looked around and at once noticed that he was stranded on some desolate plain. Miles of rough, cracked rocky ground surrounded him. The last thing he could remember was tumbling through a void of flashing lights and intense gravitational convulsions.

He stood up and surveyed the area more closely. There seemed to be nothing around for miles. The only thing that stood out was a massive mountain range that sat miles away from him. The sky above was dark and cloudy with weird bolts of electricity searing across it causing weird colors to be reflected down.

The air was cold as ice and it was eerily quiet, but suddenly he heard the sound of wheels turning. He turned and saw what appeared to be a horse-drawn carriage approaching. There was only one horse and it looked sickly and emaciated. The driver didn't look much better. He was hunched over and his clothes were tattered and torn. The wagon the horse was pulling seemed to be piled with dead, rotting corpses. The wagon pulled up slowly and the driver turned to Jason.

"You dead?"

"Uh, I don't think so. No."

"Oh," he said with disappointment.

"What are you?"

"This is the meat wagon. I pick up the strays."

"The strays. Where am I?" Jason asked. The driver lifted the brim of his moth eaten hat and looked down on him with distinct interest.

"You're from Earth, aren't you?"

"Yes."

"Okay. For your frame of reference this place is called the Unworld. This is the exact center of the universe and the place where all the big decisions are made."

"What decisions?"

"About the universe. Catch up! All the deities and gods who hold dominion over the various worlds congregate here and work together to keep this thing you call the universe turning on time."

"What am I doing here?"

"Look, I don't do guided tours. I just do my job. If you want to talk to someone who can help you with whatever you need help with, head over to those mountains there. Sanctum might be able to point you in the right direction." The driver said and with one flick of his riding crop, the meat wagon continued on its eternal journey.

Jason took a deep breath and began walking toward the mountain range. After an hour of walking, he began to feel his strength returning and soon after that, he was able to fly again. He rose up into the sky and soared forward as quickly as he could.

As he flew, Jason noticed how dark and dead everything looked. Miles of barren cracked dirt extended far past his vision. It looked to be a planet of death, lacking any sign of natural life.

As Jason reached the mountain range, he rose up above the tallest peak and on the other side he saw what appeared to be some kind of gigantic table made of solid rock. He wasn't sure what he was about to see, but when he looked down, he felt curious. There was nothing but miles of rubble and fiery rock. He landed quickly and searched through the debris. He wasn't sure what had been there, but clearly whatever it was had been destroyed not too long ago. As he walked through the wreckage, he heard the sound of someone digging through rock. He hurried toward the familiar sound and soon came upon a tall, beautiful woman with large wings jutting from her back. He slowly got closer.

"Hello?" He asked. The woman turned and was startled at first.

"Who are you?"

"I'm, Spectrum. I'm from Earth."

"Wait. You were the anomaly."

"What?"

"I had seen an anomaly in The Design and we sent someone to identify it. I was led to believe you were that anomaly, but the truth is the very person I sent to stop it, was it."

"I'm sorry. I feel like I'm walking in on the middle of the movie already in progress. What are you talking about?"

"My name is Hither. I sent Sur Reel to Earth to identify and stop an anomaly I had found in The Design, the blueprint of all time. He said it was you and I believed him, but it turns out he was the anomaly all along. He somehow regained his powers, came back here and laid us out. This destruction was all his doing. He beat us. We are gods and he beat us all!"

"Sur Reel." Jason said as something in his brain flickered. "He's why I'm here. Where is he now?"

"He's gone on to The Design. With every intention of destroying it, I imagine."

"You don't seem very interested in that fact."

"He's too powerful. There's no way I can stop him."

"Maybe I can. It was my power he took." Jason confessed. Hither looked back at him with a renewed interest.

"Then perhaps you can stop him."

"You said he was heading for The Design? Where is that?"

"It's not so much a place as it's a sense. The Unworld works on a different set of rules as far as physics goes. The Design is both worlds away and right by your side at the same time. I really don't have time to give you the full run down, but if you want to go to The Design, close your eyes."

"You're not going to stab me, are you?"

"Of course not. Just close your eyes."

Jason did as he was told. Hither walked up to him and cupped his face in her hands. "Now let your mind go. Don't think about anything. Let yourself open up to the sound of creation. Feel the energy of the universe flow through you and once you feel ready, open your eyes."

Jason did as Hither instructed. He could feel the very energy of the universe flowing through him. It wasn't forceful, but it was strong. It was like some incredible force that didn't push or pull but rather guided. Jason opened his eyes and everything that had been around him was gone. He was somewhere new. He turned and saw a rocky plateau a few miles away. On top of it was what looked like a huge tree with lights strung through the branches. Jason shot up and flew straight toward it.

As he got closer, he could make out finer details of the tree. It looked old and dead. The lights in the branches weren't lights, but rather it was a long glowing cord that was tangled among the sticky, fragile limbs.

He landed just under the boughs of the tree and looked up in amazement. The light was brilliant and beautiful. It was all around him and he could feel the energy coming off of it. It was as though he was in the presence of life itself. Suddenly, the ground beneath him shook and a fist of rock formed around him and clutched him tightly.

"Didn't think you had it in ya." Sur Reel said as he slinked from out of the shadows.

"Let me go!"

"I don't think so. I'm guessing you came here to stop me."

"Yes."

"You don't even know what I'm doing."

"I've seen what you've done. I'm pretty sure whatever you're up to isn't good."

"What do you care anyway? If I succeed, everything that was going on back on your world will be erased. It'll be like it never happened."

"Why?"

"Will you behave?"

"Fine." Jason said.

"Good." Sur Reel said and then clapped his hands together. The fist of rock opened up and Jason was free.

"What are you doing?"

"Simply? I'm shutting all this down. Do you know what this is?" Sur Reel asked, pointing up to the glowing web above their heads. Jason looked up and then shrugged.

"The Design, right?"

"Yes, but do you know what it is? What it really is? This is the universe. From beginning to end. This is the blueprint of time itself. Every fiber and sinew that it is made of represents every living soul in existence from birth to death. It maps all the events and occurrences that will ultimately shape the universe into what it shall become when it takes its last gasp. I realize, being from Earth, I'm throwing some big concepts at you. Hard to believe this glowing string could be all that, right?"

"Well, yeah," Jason said. Sur Reel folded his arms behind his back and shined a warm, almost pitying smile at Jason.

"So primitive. I'm impressed you haven't had a heart attack after seeing all of this. I have come here to make things right. I have come on a mission of justice. Things have gone so far wrong, the only solution is to simply start over from scratch." Sur Reel said as he approached The Design. He reached up to one of the glowing cords and plucked a microscopic fiber from it. "This is me. The moment I began to exist. With this little scrap, I will restart The Design, but this time around, I'll call the shots. I can make it right. I will make this thing work the way it's supposed to. You want that Tyler guy? I can make that happen. Whatever you want!"

"But you're going to kill the universe."

"So, you break a few eggs."

"It's wrong. Just because things haven't gone your way doesn't mean you can just erase everything else. Maybe this was how it was supposed to be," Jason said. Sur Reel let out a gentle laugh.

"You mortals really are so very stupid. I'm a god! I actually can control things! I can make this all go away and once it is gone, I will rebuild and I will make it right." Sur Reel said as he ran toward the end of the glowing cord. He reached up again and took another fiber from The Design. It was different as it didn't glow.

"What's that?"

"This is the end of time. The Great Darkness. This is the end of all existence. Just imagine what happens when I put this over there, next to the Big Bang."

"You can't."

"I most certainly can." Sur Reel said as he began trying to attach the dead thread to the rest of The Design. Jason leapt forward and pulled Sur Reel back, but with a soft nudge, Sur Reel sent Jason flying back.

"You're psychotic!" Jason said as he found his balance.

"You catch on fast."

"I won't let you do this." Jason said as he advanced on Sur Reel, but as quickly as that, the rock fist rose back up and threw Jason over the edge.

Jason landed on the ground below and gasped to reclaim his breath. As he got up, the rock below him began to shift and move. A large rock creature rose up and towered over him.

"Living rock, my friend! This is what I can do! Kill him, Rocky." Sur Reel shouted from above. The rock creature looked down and slammed its giant fist down on the ground. Jason leapt clear of the impact, but the rock monster was quick as it followed him.

Just as Jason was able to get his bearings, he had to jump clear of the rock monster's pounding fist again and again. Jason finally shot back up into the air and he looked down to see the rock monster jumping up, attempting to grab him. Jason looked back to Sur Reel and he could see that he was busy manipulating The Design. Jason shot forward, but as he did, the rock monster leapt up abnormally high and caught him in its fist. The monster fell back to the ground and slammed Jason down hard.

Jason pulled free from the monster's grip and ran as fast as he could, but the rock monster was on him almost instantly. Jason fell back and as he hit the ground, he shot out a beam of energy from both hands and the beams tore into the monster's torso. Just then, Jason felt a solid connection with the beams. It felt as though they had become extensions of his own body. He could feel them turning and pushing inside the rock monster's body and that's when he realized what he had to do.

Jason focused on the beams and amped up the power. The beams grew brighter and the monster seemed to finally notice the pain as they bored through its body. Jason closed his eyes and slowly pulled his arms away from each other and as he did, the beams split and began pushing and tearing through the monster's frame. With one final jerk, Jason spread his arms wide and at the same time, the beams tore the rock monster into rubble.

Jason got up quickly and shot back up to The Design, but as he arrived, he saw Sur Reel finish his work and seconds later; the divine glow of The Design began to drain away. The once brilliant fibers were growing dark and before he knew it, the entire thing had died.

"Oh. You survived." Sur Reel said with surprise as he turned back around. "You know. I misjudged you. I take it all back. If you still want in on this, I'd be happy to have you."

"You killed it."

"Focus here. I'm handing you a once in a lifetime chance. For the second time. Don't be stupid." Sur Reel said.

"You're a murderer. You are nothing more than a common murderer," Sur Reel quickly raised his arm and slapped Jason hard enough to send him sliding across the dirt.

"I am, by no means, 'common'!" Sur Reel hissed. "Now, the way I see it you have a choice to make now. Get on board with my re-imagining of the universe, or join the rest of it in the dark oblivion. If you ask me, it's a pretty easy choice."

"There is one more option." Jason said as he got up and rallied from Sur Reel's surprisingly strong blow.

"And what would that be?"

"I just stop you here and now!" Jason barked as he shot forward like a bullet. He rammed right into Sur Reel and dragged him to the ground. They slid across the dirt, kicking up dust and rock. Sur Reel got up quickly, but Jason was on him in a flash. He pounded him with his fists at a frenzied pace. Sur Reel seemed unaffected and brushed Jason aside as though he were nothing more than an impetuous child.

"Okay. I'll take that as your answer. Sorry we couldn't meet on this issue. It really would have been incredible."

"I think I'll be just fine," Jason said.

"What makes you think that?" Sur Reel asked with a giddy curiosity. Jason raised his hand up and revealed the small bit of glowing thread in his grip.

"This is you, right? Your moment of creation?"

"Give that to me!" Sur Reel demanded. Jason leapt up quickly. He looked down at the glowing thread and noticed that it was beginning to dim until eventually, it died. As the light left it, Spectrum saw Sur Reel begin to disintegrate before his eyes. "No!" Sur Reel screamed as he disappeared into a cloud of dust. A sharp, cold breeze blew through and carried what was left of him away. Jason was left there alone. He stared up at the once brilliant branches of the dead tree that seemed a bit more dead to him.

"Thank you!" A voice called from above. Jason turned and he saw Hither approaching, her wings flowing gracefully with her frame. She fell gently to the ground and greeted Jason with a warm smile. "You have succeeded."

"He killed it. I stopped him, but he killed the universe. Which makes me wonder why we're still here. Shouldn't we be ash by now?"

"This plane exists within its own reality."

"So, we're okay but everything else is toast."

"I am sorry."

"Sorry!? Where the hell am I going to go now? My world is gone. Everyone I know is dead now! My friends. My family. Tyler," Jason said. Hither was staring up at The Design and seemed intent on the once brilliant construct.

"It all happens for a reason."

"What?" Jason asked. Hither quickly turned her attention to Jason.

"It's difficult to talk about concepts such as death when you're talking about the universe. It's a living thing, true, but it's not something that can just be killed. It's far more powerful than that. It is energy, and as you know, energy cannot be destroyed."

"What are you talking about?" Hither smiled warmly at him and carefully took his hands into her own.

"Follow me," she said as she led Jason over to The Design. She carefully placed his hands upon the dormant threads. "Now concentrate. Picture what matters to you. Don't think, just feel."

"Why?"

"Just do it." Hither insisted. Jason closed his eyes and curled his fingers around the fine threads of The Design. He let his mind go. As he did, he felt the suit shift and something was beginning to happen. He could feel energy welling up inside his body, but as it grew stronger, he could feel it being drawn out. He also felt energy being drawn in at the same time. Soon the sensation intensified and it was as though two streams of energy were surging through his body, going both in and out. His mind started to flood with voices and visions of things he had never seen or heard before. His body tensed up and everything he was feeling began to intensify. Jason wasn't sure if he could contain the power that was tearing through him. His heart was racing and he felt as though he was about to explode. Suddenly, a calming, familiar voice reached through the chaos.

"Sweetheart." He heard his mother say. Soon he could see her face in front of him. He could see his parents together watching him open his Christmas presents on his first Christmas. Then they were standing behind him as he blew the candles off his tenth birthday cake. Every moment and feeling he had ever experienced seemed to be roaring back through his soul. The depth of these new sensations was unlike anything he had ever felt before. It was almost too much. He tried to loosen his fingers, but they were numb.

Jason then began to see more. He could see Tyler. It was the first day they met. He could feel the warm air and smell the faint scent of cigarettes that always haunted the main quad at the Blue Haven Community College campus. It was more than reliving a memory. It was as though Jason were feeling it for the first time, but only more deeply. He saw Tyler's face right in front of him. Their first kiss. His lips touched Jason's. They were soft and tangy. He felt the euphoria of their connection. The happiness. It was almost too much.

Jason's body began to convulse and his vision started to blur into a bright, white light and with one final push of power, he felt himself being thrown back. Jason opened his eyes and found himself on the ground. He got up quickly and as he did, he looked up to find that The Design was re-igniting. The dead strands were beginning to shine again with the divine aura of life. Soon, the entire construct was back, more brilliant than before.

"It's back." Jason said in amazement.

"Yes. Beautiful, isn't it?"

"You don't seem very moved by this. I mean, the universe could have been wiped out forever."

"It might have been."

"Might have been? You saw it!"

"You have to understand, unless it's within The Design, it's not going to happen."

"What is the deal with this thing?"

"This is the blueprint of time itself. From the moment of creation to the last moment before total oblivion. Every moment. Every life. Every last detail."

"But what about free will? Is everything all plotted out and decided before we even get up to bat?"

"There are certain events in the evolution of the universe that must happen. Without question or debate. These things must occur, however how we reach those moments can be varied. For every one point, there are an infinite ways it can be reached. For some, the direct route is chosen, but for others, it's not so simple." Hither said as she turned to Jason. She took his hands and held them tightly in hers. "Someone may have a certain specific plan in mind for their life, but something can happen that diverts them from their goal and they find a totally new path branch out before them and that will set them upon a new journey they might not have known about, but one they must take," she said. She let go of Jason's hands and looked up at the complicated weaving of The Design above. "Look upon it. See how it changes," she said. Jason looked up and just then noticed it was changing. As he looked up at it, he could see some threads shrink away while others were growing out from others. "Ever changing. Ever evolving. Every choice you make and every action you perform shifts The Design, but we are all traveling on the same path to the same destination."

"And that destination would be?"

"Not for you to know."

"So what about Sur Reel? Is he gone?"

"Unfortunately, I don't think so. I'm sure he was reconstituted somewhere within The Design. He is still a child of the universe and his energy is as precious and important as anyone else's, but between you and me, I hope he got reformed into a fire hydrant." Hither said with a smile.

"So now what?"

"Now you go home."

"Then what?"

"I don't understand. What do you mean?"

"What do I do with this suit?"

"You've been given a great gift. You now possess a great deal of power and what you choose to do with it is your own decision. The only advice I can give you is if you truly want to do what is right, listen to what your soul asks of you. It's the deepest, most essential part of you."

"But what if..."

"I can't tell you what the future holds for you. There are no absolutes. No promises. You just have to go from this place with what you've learned and simply do the best you can. The Design seems to think you are worthy of this gift. That in itself is not to be taken lightly."

"How much of this am I going to remember?"

"None of it, I'm afraid. You've done well, though. You've honored your station and for this you shall be rewarded."

"Station? What are you talking about? What reward?"

"Anything you want." Hither said. "We shall grant you any request you may have. One wish."

"A wish. I can wish for anything?"

"Anything."

"Like, I could wish that I never got this suit and none of this ever happened?"

"If that's what you want, but I don't think that it is." Hither said. Jason looked away from her as he attempted to capture his thoughts. A wish. Anything he wanted, but there were so many things he did want. He then realized the one thing he truly needed.

"Save him. I don't care how, just save him."

"Are you sure? This is a one time offer."

"I'm sure."

"He means that much to you." Jason looked up at Hither and he felt the tears form in his eyes.

"He's my world."

"Very well. It is done. Good luck, Jason Randwulf."

Hither gently placed her hand upon Jason's shoulders and light emanated from her touch. Soon the glow was so bright, everything went white.

When his vision came back, Jason discovered he was out of the Spectrum suit and back on his roof surrounded by half the Towers City Police force. His memory of the past few hours faded quickly and soon all he could worry about were the growing number of policemen advancing upon him.

"Freeze!" A voice from one of the choppers blared. "You are under arrest. Do not move or we will open fire. Lethal force has been authorized."

Jason stepped back as the copters closed in. The laser sights from the rifles the troops inside were packing danced through the night sky all around him.

"I'm sorry," Tyler said. Jason turned and saw Tyler walking toward him, and just past him, Jason saw Dave storm out. He was holding a rather large gun and had both hands gripped around the trigger. Jason was about to suit up, but suddenly everything stopped. Tyler's eyes rose to the sky and soon everyone was in a state of confusion. Jason looked up and there he was. Spectrum, floating high above the scene. With a simple wave, he greeted everyone and in a blink of an eye, he disappeared behind a flash of white light.

Everything went into slow motion. An awkward sense of confusion fell upon everyone.

"What the hell was that?" Dave asked.

"That was proof that you were wrong." Tyler said.

"We have DNA proof!"

"Yes, but how the hell could Jason be Spectrum when we just saw him fly by us a few seconds ago? Are you going to believe DNA or your own damn eyes!?"

"But..." Dave said, floundering.

"All units. Fall back. Repeat. All units. Fall back." Tyler said into his radio. He walked up to Dave and put his hand on his shoulder.

"You made a mistake,"

The copters above quickly flew back to where they came from and everything quieted down very quickly. Tyler turned to Jason and their eyes locked. "Sorry about all this."

"It's okay," He watched Tyler and Dave go back inside and once the last crackle of a police radio faded from the area, Jason began to breathe again.

He walked over to the edge of the roof and looked out at the city before him. He didn't know what had happened and he didn't know why it had happened, but it had filled him with a sense of elation and happiness. He felt as though he had been handed a second chance and he couldn't wait to make the most of it in the future.

24

The next day, Jason woke up feeling more refreshed and rejuvenated than he thought he would. He reasoned the stress of being a wanted man, at least for a little while, was enough to stress him out which aided his rest.

He got out of bed and switched on the television. The news was on and it wasn't a surprise to find that all anyone could talk about was the madness of the previous night. Jason watched as they began replaying footage from a press conference from earlier that morning where Police Chief Kelvin publicly apologized to not only Towers City, but also Jason Randwulf himself. They even had Dave come on and offer his apologies as well. His bravado was gone and he looked like a meek puppy approaching his angered master after leaving a mess on the floor. Jason smiled a bit. To see Dave so humbled and exposed was quite satisfying, but he didn't have time to gloat. He was already late for work.

As Jason pushed through the doors of the cafe, he was shocked to discover that the place was nearly filled to capacity. As he walked in, many of the patrons turned to him and started to applaud.

"What is all this about?" Jason asked as he reached the counter where Tristan was busy helping customers.

"You're a celebrity. You were singled out in a citywide manhunt.

Don't ask me. People think anyone mentioned in the news is a big star. I'm just riding the wave of notoriety. Now go get your apron on and start mingling with your people,"

It was a good day at the Lauvre Cafe. So good, in fact, Tristan actually had to ask Jason to stay longer than normal, which was fine by him.

At about noon, the crowd became more manageable and Jason was able to breathe as he went about his daily chores.

Jason was wiping down a table when he looked up and saw Heather walk in.

"Heather! You're out!"

"I told you bail wouldn't be a problem," she said as she hugged him. She then quickly pulled him aside to an empty corner of the cafe. "So?"

"So what?"

"How did you do it?"

"Do what?"

"The other Spectrum! How did you manage that?"

"Honestly? I have no idea. I was about to bust the suit out before he showed up."

"You don't think there's another one out there?"

"I don't think so. It may have been a fluke."

"Still. Good trick."

"I'm just glad it's over."

"I don't think it's over. I've been in meetings with lawyers almost constantly since I was locked up. All I can say is Manicore has a major mad on for you and Spectrum. This police thing may have blown over, but I don't think Manicore is going to disappear as easily."

"I'll worry about that later. I'm just glad to be free and not on the run."

"Me too." Heather said as she gave Jason another quick hug.

"And I'm real sorry about the police and your father getting fired."

"It's fine. My dad was going to retire this year anyway. And as far as my legal dealings, don't worry. I made sure some very high security stuff was in the shot on that security cam footage. I have a feeling they're going to drop the charges, unless Manicore wants some of their best hidden secrets paraded around in a big court case."

"Wow. Do you ever stop thinking?"

"Not really, no. I gotta go. I'll see you later."

"Sure thing," Heather skipped out the door and the feeling of rightness with the world came over Jason once more.

At the end of his shift, Jason walked out of the cafe and was headed down the street, but he was stopped suddenly as Tyler came up behind him. He was in his uniform, looking handsome as ever.

"Hey," he said.

"Tyler. Hi. I would have thought you would have taken the day off after last night."

"I should have, but I kind of had to get out. Get back into my life to clear my head."

"Are you sure it's all right for you to meet me like this? What about Dave?"

"Who I spend time with isn't really Dave's business anymore. He and I broke up last night."

"I'm sorry," Tyler smiled slightly.

"No, you're not."

"You're right. I'm not, but still, if it hurts you, I'm sorry for that."

"No. I'm fine. To be honest I felt it coming a long time ago. We just were never really on the same wavelength on a lot of things. I'm just trying to figure out how I'm going to spend my evenings from now on."

"Maybe I could help you. If you wanted to come by my place tonight. We could talk."

"I'd like that. I get off at eleven. If that's not too late."

"It's perfect. I'll have the coffee ready." Jason said with a smile. He turned and headed down the street, but he suddenly felt a hand grip his arm and pull him back. Jason found himself falling into Tyler's embrace.

"It was you, wasn't it?"

"Huh?"

"Spectrum. You're Spectrum."

"No. You saw for yourself."

"I don't buy it," Tyler said. Jason quickly pulled himself free.

"What makes you think I'm Spectrum?"

"I just know you. I just always thought if anyone could ever wind up as some kind of superhero, flying around saving the day, it would have to be you." Tyler said as he moved in closer to Jason.

"Is this some kind of sting? You get me to admit it and I'm locked up in some metal cage someplace?"

"It's true."

"Yes," Jason said. Tyler just smiled at the revelation.

"See? No cage. No sting. You're a hero."

"If that's how you want to see it."

"It is. And the hero always gets the girl." Tyler said out of the side of his mouth.

"What?"

"In all the movies and books. The hero gets the girl, doesn't he?"

"Yes. But, it's kind of different here. No girl."

"No, I guess not. We'll just have to improvise." Tyler said and then he slowly pressed his lips to Jason's. A spark shocked through the air as their grip on each other tightened. Jason felt as though a piece of him he had lost years ago finally had been found and returned and at last, he felt complete.

Epilogue

Irving Bateman had moved to Towers City thirty years ago after he had graduated from college. He hadn't anticipated spending so many years of his life there, but as his career in advertising took off, he found his desire to leave dwindle.

Soon, he met Joan, the woman who would turn out to be his wife and after their first year of marriage, his life seemed to really take off.

Their kids had grown strong and well within the city. They went to the best schools, had all the advantages and were what some considered privileged because of it.

The years drifted by with little notice and it just seemed like a steady climb up for Irving and his family.

The only moment when Irving may have considered leaving Towers was when the news started reporting the appearance of a super hero. Irving didn't have a good feeling about Spectrum. He wasn't comfortable allowing one person with such power to be anywhere around him or his family. Such characters were known to attract trouble of all kinds, but after a few weeks and seeing how calm things remained, Irving thought that maybe he was wrong. '

On Monday morning, Irving woke up in their penthouse apartment. It was as though he were waking up there for the first time. They had just completed an extensive remodeling of the entire unit. It was a goal of his for years and after finally making partner two years ago, he was finally able to make it a reality.

He and Joan designed and planned every aspect of their new home from the smallest detail to the biggest piece of furniture. The kitchen had custom chrome accents and imported Italian marble counters. The bathroom was decorated with the finest pottery from Africa and South America. The hardwood floors were polished to perfection and the furniture had been hand made in Paris.

Their home was a culmination of their tastes and their success in life. It was a monument to everything they ever wanted.

Irving pulled himself out of bed and surveyed the master bedroom through his sleepy eyes. It was still dark because they preferred to keep the blinds shut all day long. He padded out to the living room and as he did, he heard the coffee maker switch on and soon the aroma of an exclusive Brazilian blend filled the air.

Irving walked up to one of the large sliding doors that opened up to their patio, which featured an Olympic sized pool. He pulled the curtains open and expected to be bathed in the rays of the morning sun, but there was no warmth. He looked up and saw the sky was dark and the light from the sun had been blotted out. Not by clouds, but by large severe looking space ships. There were hundreds of them filling the sky above Towers City. Some small, others were large. They were hovering over the city in some kind of pattern.

"Honey!" He called out. "I think we should move!"

CPSIA information can be obtained at www.ICGtesting.com
Printed in the USA
BVOW02s0524121213

338883BV00002B/22/P